PORTAL-LAND, OREGON

STEFON MEARS

Thousand
Faces
Publishing

Also by Stefon Mears

Published by Thousand Faces Publishing, Portland, Oregon

http://1kfaces.com

Copyright © 2019 by Stefon Mears

Front cover image © Grandfailure | Dreamstime.com

ISBN: 978-0-9977924-9-2

1

PORTLAND. THEY TELL YOU IT'S WEIRD. THEY DON'T TELL YOU it's *wyrd*.

'Course, most people don't know the difference. Not really. I sure didn't. No, right up until the day I found out the truth, I was just another California expatriate running away to the Pacific Northwest.

I didn't do it to steal a job, though, or blow up the housing market.

I fled the Bay Area because of a breakup.

Kind of stupid, when I look at it that way. But it's the kind of thing you do when you're twenty-four and your whole world has come crashing down.

Katy. She was the world that came crashing down.

Six months in, I was sure she was The One. By the one-year mark, I was confident we were headed for marriage, the house, the kids, the dog, the whole nine. I'd even started saving for the wedding, in a special surprise account.

Wasn't just because Katy was beautiful, either, with her soap commercial skin and big blue eyes. We had the same taste in science fiction and fantasy, the same love of horror films. She didn't like some of my music, but that was all right. I didn't like most of her New Age crap.

I figured those little differences were what made relationships last.

The truth hit me like a rancid pie in the face.

Katy, big blue eyes full of tears. Apologizing and begging my forgiveness even as she was packing her bags to split town for Sedona, Arizona, of all places.

Turned out she'd met her "twin flame" in some internet chatroom.

Obviously that meant she was destined to dump my ass and run off to start her life anew with him.

I didn't know what a "twin flame" was. Still don't, now that I think of it. I think Katy tried to tell me during her blubbering *mea maxima culpa* explanation, but the truth is, all I could hear was my own blood rushing past my ears, and a crashing sound like a truck full of cymbals getting sideswiped by a plane full of hi-hats.

And then was she was gone, and the apartment looked half-again too big. And not just that. Everything in my life looked wrong then.

The job I'd been so happy with? Just a grind that would eat my soul.

The friends I loved so well? Well, they were the same people I loved, but now they all gave me the *look*.

If you've never seen the *look*, good for you. Closest I can come to describing it is a blend of sympathy, pity, and condescension.

As though they'd all seen this coming, but none of them could have been bothered to tell me.

I wasn't sure which part of the *look* was worse, the pity, or the condescension. Didn't matter. I couldn't take either very long. I needed space, and I needed it now.

Katy was out the door maybe three days before I was online, hunting up an apartment in Portland, Oregon.

Why Portland?

I don't like L.A., Seattle gets too much snow for me, and I wasn't leaving the West Coast.

Portland seemed to have the perfect combination of forest and city. Plus, they had a thriving live music scene. And Powell's, of course.

The chance to live that close to that many books?

Sealed the deal.

It was three weeks After Katy when I'd moved into a little apartment just inside the Beaverton border, on the northwest edge of Portland.

Six weeks A.K., I found out that Portland wasn't named for its port.

It was a beautiful May morning. A Saturday, which meant pretty much everyone in the area was asleep or outside.

Much rain as we got, seeing the sun on a spring weekend was like found money. Couldn't wait to blow it.

For me, it finally meant a chance to check out the quality of pickup basketball in Riverfront Park.

Riverfront Park is kind of what it sounds like. A great big strip of grass — acres, really — plunked down on the west bank of the Willamette River. Throw in a fountain, concrete areas for events, a hiking trail around the edges, some basketball courts, and a whole mess of trees, benches and the like, and on sunny days the place got downright crowded.

Birthday parties, elaborate frisbee games, roughly three kennels worth of happy dogs, plus a soupcon of joggers, bikers, and old folks just getting their steps.

Not to mention the great big Saturday Market, where locals artists, farmers, and others all came to hawk their wares.

Sprinkle all that liberally with homeless people, and you have Riverfront Park in the spring.

I was there for the basketball, though, and what I found made me very happy.

Wasn't there twenty minutes before I ended up running pickup full-court five-on-five with a bunch of guys and gals who were as good as any I'd played against. And I'd been playing pickup basketball since I was big enough to throw the ball through the hoop.

This was the best kind of game, really.

Well, *almost* the best. My team had just lost twenty-three to twenty-one. May not sound like much, but each basket was worth one point, and it was a contest to fifteen, except you had to win by two. Throw in some trash talk and energetic defense, and we'd been running hard for a half-hour solid. Easy.

As I said. Good games, at Riverfront Park.

Unfortunately, losing meant going to the end of the line. We'd be out for the better part of an hour, unless another team came up short a player and drafted one of us.

And with me being the new kid on the block, I wasn't going to be the one drafted. Killer jump shot or not.

So I left my teammates to gaze hopefully at the incoming team, and flopped on the thick grass near the edge of the court, a panting pile of sweat, made decent by a blue-and-gold U. C. Monterey tee shirt and gray shorts.

Gentle breeze off the Willamette kissed my face, carrying the kind of clean river smells I wasn't used to. The closest I knew to rivers growing up in the Bay Area were the cement creeks that cut through my home town of Long Pine City.

The creeks smelled like moss and decay, an association that only built during my four years in Monterey, right on the Pacific.

But here, the Willamette smelled downright refreshing. Or maybe I was just that tired. Or that thirsty.

The sun beat down on me, as I listened to good-natured razzing while the current teams exchanged shots from the top of the key, to establish first possession.

The combination of sun-heat and exercise-heat a miasma that clung to my skin.

I dumped water on my face, still icy cold thanks to my Costco-special thermos. Some kind of space shuttle metal, but still heavy as lead when it was full of water.

Needed both hands to invert that beast above my face. Some of the water got into my mouth, and I gulped it down gratefully as I stopped the deluge.

Didn't just cool me off. Got the sting of sweat out of my eyes, and the taste of sweat off my tongue. Drove away the feeling that I was emanating stink lines.

Plus, it wasn't as though my short blond hair was going to get *more* matted to my head.

The water didn't do anything for my hunger though, and I hadn't eaten since that oversized blueberry muffin before I left my apartment.

I was just craning my neck to glance past the game and judge how far I was from the food tents over at the Saturday Market, when I heard the sound that changed my life.

A cry for help.

THE CRY WAS A SINGLE WORD.

"Help!"

A woman's voice. Young-sounding. A nice voice, too, like she'd sing mezzo soprano.

I heard that cry, and it was like the whole world just froze.

The joggers, the birthday parties, the cars going up and down Naito, the Saturday Market, even the two full courts of raucous basketball. Frozen.

Even the air seemed to stop moving.

A moment between heartbeats that just stretched out, while what I'd heard sank into my head.

A cry for help.

An *urgent* cry for help.

When I heard it I was sprawled on the Riverfront Park grass, just off the basketball courts. My limbs tired, but the good kind of tired. Workout tired, like they'd be ready to go again if I gave them some rest first. Fifteen minutes or so. My whole body drenched with sweat, where I hadn't splashed it away with water from my heavy thermos.

The hot sun high above, but not yet noontime high. Wasn't 'til later I found out I'd heard that cry at exactly eleven-eleven and eleven seconds a.m. Later still 'til I found out why that mattered.

Then my heart beat again. Movement and sound came back to the world.

I jumped to my feet. Looked at my despondent teammates, stuck waiting for a game like I was. All their attention on the game in front of them.

I didn't know any of their names. Typical pickup situation. The muscled Latina was Shorty. The big guy with the fro was Jolly, as in Green Giant. I was real-world tall, but this guy was basketball tall. The freckled guy was Red for his hair. The other guy was Metallica, for his tee shirt.

Same reason they called me Monterey, instead of Scott. My shirt. I'd probably have to play here at least three times before anyone bothered to learn my name.

Assuming the courts were still here. They weren't year-round.

"Guys," I said. "You hear that?"

Not one looked away from the game. Shorty shook her head. Jolly just mentioned a weakness he spotted in a team's defense of the pick-and-roll.

"Someone needs help," I prompted.

One big guy *might* chase off a problem, but three or four big guys definitely could.

Only Red looked at me, and he frowned like I was crazy.

I was on my own then.

The cry came again. Sharper. Terrified.

I was gone. Grabbed my keys and thermos and started sprinting toward the sound.

Not easy to track a single word in a place as noisy as Riverfront Park on a Saturday morning in May. But I was sure I heard the cry coming from closer to the river.

Off the courts I ran. Head craning. Looking for trouble.

Across a concrete area.

Young mother with two kids in a stroller. No trouble there.

Homeless guy sprawled and snoozing with his dog. No trouble

Past the bathrooms.

Nothing but casual strollers. A few relaxed couples gazing out at the river or at each other.

Hot concrete under my sneakers. Cool, river-wet breeze in my face.

But no sign of someone in trouble.

I reached the waist-high fence that was all that stood between me and the Willamette. Well, that and a drop of twenty feet or so. The fence was dirty steel rails between short, thick, concrete pylons.

I whipped my head back and forth.

Nothing.

In a park as crowded as this one, I now stood in a region maybe the size of a half-court, where I was the only person. Nearest pedestrians, all strolling away.

All moving away. No one coming this way.

No one else coming to help?

But help who?

"I'm here to help," I called out. Desperate. "Where are you?"

"Here!"

Same voice. Same urgency.

In the water?

The rail was hot against my hips as I craned over, scanning for the sight of a woman overboard. Wondering how far it was to the nearest point anyone could get out of the river.

I knew people swam in the Willamette. There had to be places...

The Portland Spirit. A cruise ship that went up and down the river. Its dock was no more than a couple of hundred yards from...

Movement.

A head, breaking the water.

An otter's head?

It was a big otter. Maybe five feet long. But it was definitely an otter.

"Please!" the otter cried out in that mezzo soprano voice. "It's too fast for me!"

My mouth opened so wide I'm pretty sure my jaw bounced off my collarbone. I almost started looking around the for the camera, because this *had* to be a joke.

But the otter's eyes narrowed. Its voice got all the more desperate as it said, "Please."

I nodded. What else was there to do? It may have been a talking otter, but it needed help.

The otter pointed behind it, then started swimming to my left.

Behind the otter I saw movement under the turbulent waters of the river. A dark shadow. Maybe fifteen feet long. Coming closer.

Closer.

Consistent speed. That was good for me.

I didn't exactly have a fishing spear. I had a thermos. Not much, but it was still half-full and pretty heavy. Regular shape. Cylindrical. Wouldn't be much different from throwing a football.

I hefted the thermos.

Watched the shadow rise up. Rise up.

Break the water.

I threw before I even got a good look at the thing. I did see gray, fishy skin. A vaguely humanoid head. A whole lot of teeth.

Put my whole body into the throw. Perfect spiral. Angled to use some of the thing's momentum against it.

Completion!

My thermos clanged off the thing's skull. Too close to the sound of a basketball bouncing off a rim for my liking.

How could it sound so metallic? Shouldn't there have been a thud?

Not where my focus should have been.

I'd put all my weight into that throw. With my hips against the rail.

Over I went.

I had just long enough to yell out, "Shit!"

Splash!

Once, when I was a little kid, I had the chicken pox. Really bad case. Temp running over a hundred and five. Temp that high, I'd started hallucinating. Losing touch with reality. Had no idea who these well-meaning people around me were, even though they were my brother Kenzie, my sister Rona, and my parents.

Mom had finally stuck me in an ice bath to get my temperature down.

Plunging into the Willamette was kind of like that ice bath.

Surface tension smacked my face. Cold shock of water seized up my tired limbs.

All I could do to keep my mouth shut against the need to find air. I should have sucked in a breath instead of swearing during the fall.

Wild-eyed and desperate. Lungs burning. Limbs too. Hunting the surface. Stressing the fish monster. Hoping the otter got away.

Light. I could see light.

Kicking with legs that wanted a break. Whipping arms, just as tired. Heart pounding. Lungs begging for a breath.

I broke the surface. Sucked in my body weight in air.

Spun left and right.

The fish monster. The otter. Where were they?

Gone.

2

A COUPLE OF HUNDRED YARDS SOUTH TO THE PORTLAND SPIRIT'S DECK. Sounded like next to nothing when I was standing up above, my hips against the rail.

Here in the waters of the Willamette? With my whole body half-frozen and my limbs exhausted from basketball?

Looked like the distance to Brazil.

Nothing I could do though. I started swimming.

Sure, I was using the most awkward-looking strokes ever taken by someone attempting to swim, but they were all I could manage. My legs didn't want to straighten all the way. My arms either. My whole body wanted to clench in and preserve what heat I had.

Plus, my lungs were bitching about this whole experience, and my heart was trying to settle the matter by pumping extra blood to every part of my body. Right. This. Second.

Slow, shivery and shaking, I started making headway.

I think I was probably rocketing along at the breakneck pace of a yard a minute when I heard someone call down to me.

"Hey, Jackass!"

The idea that the woman could have been talking to someone else never occurred to me.

I had to half-roll over to look up, and all my limbs pulled in immediately to try to conserve body heat.

Bad idea. I dipped under the water. I came up spitting water. Had to force my limbs into something like a treading water move so I could actually look up.

The woman calling to me was a cop. I like to think she looked more amused than disgusted.

"Yeah, you," she said. She pointed. "Try the ladder."

Sure enough, there were emergency ladders every so many feet along the edge of the river.

Not as close as I would have liked, but a hell of a lot closer than the Portland Spirit's dock.

I started that direction.

Must have taken me even longer than it felt like, because the cop called down to me again.

"You gonna make it? I can call for help."

"I-I-I c-c-c-c"

"Just swim, Jackass," she said.

I think she hefted her radio then, but I had my whole attention back on getting to the ladder.

You know. Looking back on that moment, I think that reaching and scaling that ladder may have been the single most difficult physical feat of my life. I was that cold and that drained.

Still, these days, that's saying something.

Of course, I didn't actually climb over the rail on my own. By the time I got up close enough to try, the cop had lost her patience. Or she didn't believe I could make it, which I might not have.

Either way, she grabbed me by one shoulder and the waistband of my shorts and hauled me over.

The drop to the concrete was much shorter than the drop to the river.

It hurt just about as much though.

At least, I think it did. Parts of my body were numb.

The cop threw a blanket over me. Thin, dark blue thing. Like one of those airline blankets, only larger. What warmth it gave was welcome though.

People applauded.

Wait. People saw that?

Sure enough, there was a small crowd nearby now, watching the cop save the idiot.

They didn't hear the otter crying for help. They didn't see my heroic effort at rescuing said otter. But my humiliating return to the surface? That they saw?

No justice in this world.

I huddled under the blanket on the scalding hot concrete while the cop looked at my eyes. Poked me a few places. Asked basic questions, first establishing that I wasn't critically injured, but then trying to establish that I knew what year it was and so on.

Gee, a less confident man might have thought she questioned his mental stability.

Once I'd gotten enough warmth back into my body to stop chattering with every breath — and the crowd had moved on to something more immediately interesting — the cop asked the more serious questions. Name. Place of residence. The usual.

She wasn't thrilled that I wasn't carrying I.D., but she seemed to accept my explanation about just keeping money and my MAX card in my shoe while playing basketball.

Which finally got us to the question I dreaded...

"Want to tell me why you decided to go for a dip? This isn't exactly one of the swimming docks."

There were swimming docks?

Not the time to ask that.

I looked up into her brown eyes. Now that I wasn't worried about dying, I could see that she was pretty. Dark skin, good complexion.

Of course, the look in those eyes said that I was an idiot...

"I'm not sure you'll believe me."

"Oh," she said with a smile that didn't have a lot of humor to it, "now I *know* I want to hear this."

"Someone was calling for help."

"Who?" she said, immediately alert and raising up the mic of her portable radio. "Is there someone else down there?"

"No," I said, shaking my head. "Honest. I was wrong. I thought I'd heard a woman call for help but ... there was no woman."

For some reason, I couldn't bring myself to tell the nice lady cop that I'd heard an *otter* crying for help.

"And you decided to jump in anyway?"

"I didn't mean to. While I was at the rail, I ... well, I saw an otter. And I thought it looked like it was about to get eaten by a..." — *don't say fish monster, Scott, don't say fish monster* — "shark—"

"No sharks in this river. The Columbia, yeah, sometimes, but not the Willamette."

"That was what it looked like to me. So I threw my thermos at what I thought was a shark, and—"

"And you overbalanced and fell in."

I gave her an embarrassed smile.

And for the first time, I got a smile back. A little one, but still. It was the first expression I'd seen from her that said anything other than "Jackass."

"Well," she said, giving me a hand and helping me to my feet, "anyone who'd do something that stupid to try to save an otter can't be all bad."

"Thanks," I said.

"*But*," she added, raising a warning finger, "let's try to avoid doing that again, shall we? Last thing we need is good Samaritans drowning like idiots."

"Right," I said, chastened. Embarrassed again, even though warmth was seeping back into me. The warmth wasn't enough though. My whole body was exhausted to the point that I wanted to lie back down on the warm concrete and just rest.

Plus, my stomach was screaming loud enough for food that my legs had started shaking in sympathy.

"You gonna be all right if I walk away now? You don't look like you need an ambulance. Meal and a cup of coffee maybe. Still. Need me to call somebody?"

"Don't really know anybody yet. Not local."

She shook her head. "You're from Cali, aren't you?"

I winced at her use of the word "Cali." In the Bay Area, that's considered just shy of a hate crime. Like calling SF "Frisco."

"Thought so," she said, shaking her head at my wince. "Well, if you're here visiting, enjoy yourself, but be careful. If you moved here, best learn a thing or two about the outdoors, or Oregon will eat you alive."

"Thank you, Officer..."

"Martinez," she said, and this time I was pretty sure her smile was amusement. "Maria Martinez."

"Thank you, Officer Maria Martinez," I said, bowing from the neck.

I whipped the blanket off with as much flourish as my tired limbs could manage. Held it out to her.

"Your blanket."

"Not mine," she said, smiling still as she shook her head. She pointed over to one side. "That gentleman was kind enough to loan it."

I looked where she was pointing.

A homeless man, sitting on the bench. Watching us. On the skinny side. Deeply tanned, with wild gray hair. He wore two ancient, stained plaid shirts over at least one tee shirt. Good jeans though. Worn, but no holes or patches. And he had on decent brown hiking boots.

He had all his possessions in a duffel bag that looked older than he was, and this guy was probably pushing sixty.

He also had a dog. A little beagle, sitting at attention with its tail wagging furiously

The man nodded when I looked over. I nodded back.

Officer Martinez was walking away by this point.

"Wait," I called to her. When she looked back, I said, "Haven't seen my keys by any chance? I'm pretty sure I dropped them *before* I fell."

She shook her head and kept walking.

"I have them," the homeless man said. "Found them by the rail."

I walked over to him. His dog immediately stood and started sniffing at me. Paced all the way around me that way, sniffing all the while.

The man didn't seem to notice, though. His attention was on me. His eyes were hazel, and they had a ... quality to them. His skin might have wrinkles and his wild hair lots of gray, but his eyes could have been the eyes of a newborn.

"Thank you," I said, holding out the blanket. "I'm Scott Eagleson."

The man nodded. Looked me up and down. Stood.

He frowned. Tapped the stubble on his chin.

He took the blanket and draped it over my shoulders.

"Sit," he said, pointing to the spot where he'd just been sitting.

I noticed something then. He didn't, well, he didn't *smell* homeless.

I'd never spent much time around the homeless, but moving around the Bay Area — and especially running around the City (which is San Francisco, in case you don't know) — they're part of the background. And they pretty much always smelled dirty, sometimes of urine.

But this man, he had only a ... musky kind of smell. Clean, but more like an animal than a man.

I sat where he'd pointed.

Still frowning, he looked me over. And not at the usual kind of places. He looked just above my head. Then down at my hands. Wrists. Then my feet.

"Stick out your tongue," he said.

"I'm sorry?" I said, and my stomach seized in a growl that could probably have been heard all the way down in Monterey.

"Stick. Out. Your. Tongue. Then I'll give you something to eat."

"That's ridiculous," I said, starting to stand. "If anything, I owe *you* a meal. In fact, let's—"

He pushed me back down with a gentle, but insistent pressure.

"Tongue," he said.

His dog let out a single yap, for emphasis. The dog was sitting now, watching me with the same patient intensity as its master.

The man's eyes looked as though he could wait forever.

How much more stupid could I feel in one day?

I stuck out my tongue.

The man nodded, as though he'd seen what he expected to see. He picked up his duffel bag. He also handed me a banana, though I didn't see where he'd gotten it.

My stomach informed me that I was in no position to question the appearance of a banana. It was sweet and ripe, and I finished it so fast, the man had barely had time to start talking.

"You shouldn't open them from that end," he said. "The stem isn't a pull tab. Next time, pinch the bottom and peel from there. That's how monkeys do it in the wild."

"Can I have my keys?"

"Keys," he said with a small chuckle. "Yes. Exactly. You have more keys than you know. Walk with me."

"Look," I said, sounding just as spent as I felt. "I'm wet. I'm exhausted. I'm—

"Eat this," the man said, shoving what looked like a small, lime green gumball into my hand.

To my own amazement, I popped it into my mouth without thinking.

Tasted like key lime pie. As I chewed, warm relaxation spread through me. Not like I might fall asleep, but more like I'd just woken up after a long, much-needed rest. Every muscle in my body felt good now. Energized.

This day was just getting weirder. Talking otters? Bizarre, otter-eating fishmen? And now, what, healing gumballs?

I had lots of questions.

Before I could try asking any of them, the man turned and started walking away from the riverfront across the grass. His dog immediately fell into step beside him.

And he still had my keys.

3

RENEWED VIGOR ALL THROUGH MY SYSTEM. MY BODY FELT REFRESHED. Recharged. Awake.

Not just awake. Ready to take on the world. The blanket around my shoulders wasn't giving me critical warmth. It was a cape, and I was a superhero.

The May sun on my skin felt good now. Less important-to-stay-alive and more good-to-be-alive, if you see the distinction.

I wanted more sun. Whipped off the makeshift cape and gathered it in a quick twirl of my hands.

The fresh grass smell of the park blended well with the clean smells off the river, making me stand even straighter.

The taste of key lime still in my mouth, and my stomach pleasantly full, as though I'd eaten actual pie at the end of a good dinner.

I didn't feel like a man who'd played a half-hour-plus of intense basketball before diving into the Willamette River to save a talking otter's life. I felt more like a man who'd just woken up from a sweet dream, preceded by a good workout and an even better meal.

If it weren't for the fact that I was still sopping wet, I might have questioned my sanity as much as Officer Martinez had.

Fortunately the noontime sunshine was warm enough that even my soaked shirt, shorts and shoes would dry out before too long.

And right now, the only possible source of answers was an old homeless man with a beagle. Both of them walking away from me across the broad grassy middle of Riverfront Park.

The crowds of the park seemed to part around the old man and his dog.

The two walked straight through what looked to be a combined birthday party for three little kids. Banners, streamers, scores of running, screaming children and maybe a dozen harried adults trying to keep up.

Oh, and cakes. Three huge, half-eaten sheet cakes in different colors.

Probably the reason the kids were so manic.

And yet, the old man and his dog strode right through the center of the party, and no one even seemed to notice them.

Me, I had to take the long way around the party at a quick jog. Couldn't risk running over a tot in my haste.

I did cut through a game of fetch involving a golden retriever and an Australian shepherd, competing for the same tennis ball and having the time of their lives.

By the time I caught up with the old man and his beagle, the two of them were strolling along the sidewalk between the park grass and Naito Parkway. Bicyclists seemed to slip around them without paying them any mind.

"Good," the old man said. "I was afraid you'd decided not to join us."

"You still have my keys," I said, and the word "keys" made the old man chuckle again.

He shook his head. "Do I? Well, the physical ones, I suppose. If I give them back to you now, will you still walk with me? We have much to talk about."

"What's going—"

"I'll take that as a yes," the old man said, handing me back my keys. The beagle barked happily, as though this were some important part of his day, and he was so glad it finally arrived.

All the while the old man was setting his wicked pace along the sidewalk, and I was hustling to keep up.

I slid my keys back into my shorts pocket.

"So," I started, but the old man stopped walking next to a Portland Loo.

Portland couldn't just settle for concrete public restrooms like most parks I'd been to. No. Not Portland. They had to have these things.

The "loos" were made from ... aluminum, I thought. Maybe a dull, brushed steel. Made for one person, but wide and deep enough for wheelchair access. Indoor hand sanitizer. Outdoor hand wash, with soap, above a grate.

The inside looked like someone had pulled a toilet stall out of the Death Star and dropped it in there.

Cleaner than most? Yes. Nice to look at? Certainly. Still smelled pretty much like a public restroom.

"Now," the old man said. "In here."

My hands came up like he'd pulled a gun.

"Whoa," I said. "I'm grateful and all, but—"

"Don't be a child," he said, not looking at me. Then he mumbled something.

Odd, the words he spoke then. Didn't sound like English to me. Didn't sound like any language I'd ever heard spoken, either. I wasn't exactly a world-traveler, but I could recognize most of the Romance languages, plus German, Russian, and I could tell Chinese from Japanese.

For an American, I was practically a polyglot.

But the words that old man mumbled, they didn't make any sense to me.

Making even less sense was the way the world went still again. Just the way it had when I heard the otter call for help.

So still I even had a moment to realize how bizarre that thought was.

And yet, the air again stopped moving. The cars on Naito. The joggers. The bicyclists. Even the young gay couple holding hands as they passed us. The beagle's tail.

No movement. Just a kind of silent pressure to the air.

Then my heart beat again.

The world leapt back to life. Movement. Sound. All as though nothing had happened.

I tried to ask what just happened, but the question died on my lips.

The old man opened the door to the Portland Loo. Greenish light blazed out of it.

Inside, now, was not a toilet, but a hallway. White marble floor. Tan stucco walls and ceiling. A light trim of red flowered wallpaper at waist height. The soft strains of Mozart leaked out, along with the smell of roses.

"Come along now," the old man said. "Your answers are this way."

He turned and walked through the doorway. The old man who had still not given me his name.

The beagle cocked his head at me. Barked three short yaps, then turned and followed his master, nails clicking on the marble.

The hallway stood before me, its green glow now only just edging onto the sidewalk.

My heart pounded with shock greater than watching an otter speak English.

This was it. Right here. I could feel it.

Right now, I could turn away, if I wanted to. Forget about the English-speaking otter. The strange fish monster. Forget even that the nameless old man had somehow made a Portland Loo open up into a marble freaking hallway.

Walking away would be the smart choice. The sane choice. I knew that. I could feel it in my guts.

But I'd done the smart thing all my life. The safe thing. The sane thing. Even running away to Portland I only did because I had enough in the "wedding fund" to cover me while I got my life together.

But where had safe and sane gotten me?

Dumped by the love of my life. Looked down on by my friends. Desperate enough for change to just pick up my life and move it hundreds of miles north.

On the other hand, just today I'd met a talking otter. Saved it from a fish monster.

And now, I was staring at real, honest-to-God magic.

I stepped into that hallway and closed the door behind me.

IT WAS REAL. IT WAS ALL REAL.

I have to admit, when I stepped through the door of that Portland Loo, I half expected to find myself inside, well, a Portland Loo. A space that would have felt altogether cramped with me, the old man, and his dog.

Yes, I knew what it had looked like. Yes, I was ready to believe it was magic. But being ready to believe and getting confirmation, those were two different things.

But the moment I stepped through that green, glowing doorway, I was surrounded by the light fragrance of roses. I closed the door and the strains of a Mozart sonata replaced the raucous noises of Riverfront Park and Naito Parkway.

And I was standing on a white marble floor. Cool to the touch. I know that, because I bent right down and touched it with my fingers.

The marble was wide enough I could have lain down on it without my head or feet touching the walls, but not by much.

I didn't do that though.

I did run my fingers over the tan stucco walls and the narrow strip of rose-covered wallpaper that ran along the walls at waist height.

I looked up at more brown stucco. A ceiling no more than ten feet up. Low enough I could jump up and touch it if I wanted.

So I did that too.

I started laughing. I don't even know why. Maybe it was just all too much too fast. I just know that I stood there, one step inside that thick, brown oak door — not the metal door I'd felt my hand close, by the way — and started laughing like a little kid who woke up to discover it was Christmas morning.

"Come along," the old man called from further down the hallway. "You have a lot more to see."

His beagle came trotting back to me, nails clicking eagerly along the marble floor.

He stopped in front of me. Tail going like mad.

"It's real," I said, crouching down and scritching him between the ears while he pressed his head against my fingers. "It's all real."

The beagle barked his confirmation. Or maybe he was calling me a jackass. Tough to say. Either way, he seemed happy about it.

"Come on," the old man called from down the hall.

Still laughing, I trotted to meet him. Thrilling in the way my legs responded. Not at all tired from all that basketball or my impromptu dip in the Willamette. No, that little key lime gumball had done its work well.

Just more magic on a day that was looking up.

I caught up to the old man maybe fifty yards down the hallway, which wasn't even close to half its length. He was still walking at a brisk pace, even with that heavy duffel bag slung over one shoulder.

He accepted back his blanket when I offered it, and stuffed it in the duffel without looking.

"I'm Vasco," the old man said, smiling at me with both his eyes and his lips. "And you've already met Magellan."

The beagle, Magellan I presumed, barked a greeting.

That made me laugh again. Everything was making me laugh now. To that point that it almost worried me, but even worrying made me laugh.

"That'll pass," Vasco said. "The laughing. You're adjusting."

"To" — chuckle — "what?"

"The energies." Vasco gestured around himself. "You used a portal for the first time. That's a heady experience. And you did it soon after taking a restorer, and that was possibly too soon after your experience in the river."

Magellan barked.

"I said it was possibly too soon," Vasco said, sounding a little irritated. "Magellan thinks you'd have done better with a ham sandwich than a restorer. But I wanted to make sure you were up to accompanying us without getting sick. You wouldn't want to go through a portal with a head cold. Especially not your first time."

I imagined laughing and sneezing at the same time, and that just got me laughing hard enough I had to stop and put my hands on my knees.

Magellan ran back and forth between Vasco and me, barking.

"Oh," Vasco said, addressing the beagle, "so now you *want* me to do something about his condition. You're the one who thought the restorer might be too much for him."

Magellan yipped back a five-sequence that somehow sounded both displeased and superior.

"Honestly," Vasco said to me. "He learns a few things about alchemy and thinks he knows better than I do."

That just got me laughing again.

"Fine," Vasco said. He stepped right up to me. "Look at me."

I had to stand up straight. First time I noticed that Vasco was almost as tall as I was. I also noticed then that he only had one flannel shirt on after all, the red, and it wasn't ratty in the least.

"Scott. Angus. Eagleson."

It was just my name, but something in the way Vasco said it made the three parts of my name resonate right through my whole system.

The vibrations seemed to work their way right into my spine. Up past my head, then down past my feet, then up again to somewhere around my solar plexus. When the vibrations got there, they seemed to explode in all directions at once.

I shook myself. Wide awake and sober as a nun.

"What did you do?"

"Cheated," Vasco said with a mysterious smile. "Maybe I'll show you how someday."

Vasco turned and started walking back down the hall. I had to hurry to catch up with him.

"How did you know my middle name?"

"I'd tell you," Vasco said, his voice as teasing as his eyes, "but that would be cheating."

Finally we reached the end of that long, long hallway.

The hall ended not in another doorway, but the hall itself tapered at the top to form an archway, trimmed in black marble shot through with gold.

I couldn't see through the archway. It seemed nothing but an area of blackness. Like a whole and I frowned at that, but decided I wasn't going to bother asking. Vasco had made it more than clear that he didn't intend to answer any questions until we got wherever it was he was taking me.

So instead I drew a deep breath, let it out, and turned an expectant look on Vasco.

Vasco gave me a smile full of mischief. Magellan barked an excited triplet.

Vasco swept his arm out wide toward the blackness of the archway.

"After you."

4

WHEN I HEARD THE OTTER CALL FOR HELP, I HESITATED.

When I saw the doorway of the Portland Loo open into this long marble hallway, I hesitated.

But this time, staring at the wall of empty blackness at the end of that marble hallway, I didn't even pause.

Vasco swept out his arm wide, and I stepped right though as though it was a curtain that would part for me.

It didn't.

Passing through that shaft of darkness only took one, single step. But it was a step that seemed to take forever.

My raised foot touched the blackness. Pressed forward, and immediately...

It wasn't that there was resistance, per se. More like it was surface tension. Like I was stepping into pudding.

My foot pressed forward, and the rest of me followed. I couldn't have stopped if I'd wanted to. The moment my foot started its way through that sheet of blackness, the rest of me followed. I don't even think my muscles were involved anymore.

It was more like, touching the blackness had been my idea, but touching it meant coming through it. No backing out. No changing my mind.

And yet, moving through it wasn't fast, either.

My foot proceeded at the approximate speed of a decrepit snail. And yet it continued forward. My leg right behind it. My hand, too.

With my hand came more sensation. Cool. Gelatinous. I really did feel as though I was passing through pudding now.

All the way to my knee and arm.

All the way to my hip and shoulder.

Thirty seconds. Thirty years. I had no idea how long it too just to get that far. My hip and shoulder touching the blackness.

My nose too. I'm pretty sure I felt that weird, chilly pressure on the tip of my nose.

But that was as far as I had to get. My foot touched down on the other side—

—and just like that, I was through.

And what I saw...

I was standing at the edge of a gigantic crystal cavern. Quartz maybe, if quartz came in pretty much every color of the rainbow, including all the little shades in between.

The floor beneath my sneakers was that sort of generic, white crystal that I thought of when I thought of quartz. Albeit giving off a soft, white glow.

The walls though. I was standing at the darkest shade of red, and I could trace the pattern of the rainbow with my eyes all along the outer edge of this cavern. The very walls all seemed to glow their color from some light source inside them, all the way up to where the colors came together in a single black, glowing circle in the center of the dome high above.

And it was high, the apex of that ceiling. Easily three hundred, maybe five hundred feet up.

A quick assessment with my eyes told me that it was at least that far across this cavern too.

Not that I could have walked straight across it.

No, the cavern descended in striated levels before me. And to guess from the little I could see, each level had walls about twenty feet high, repeating the color pattern in the opposite direction of the level above it.

The floor of this level — and so probably the same for each level — was maybe fifty feet across. Even though I could hear echoes of noises that sounded like they might have been speech coming from the lower levels, I couldn't really see any movement or life yet.

Well, that wasn't quite true. I could see bats flitting around up high above. Yellowish, with black wings. Huge. Fruit bats maybe? I wasn't sure. I wasn't used to the idea of bats being so big. Or that happy anywhere there was that much light.

Bats in the Portland area, they were pretty much like bats down in the Bay Area — night dwellers, coming out to feast on the insects.

But the bats up above. They seemed to be flying for some kind of purpose other than eating. And when they reached spots on the walls, they vanished.

Watching one vanish made me jump.

"It's all right," Vasco said...

...from in front of me. He was in front of me. One hand raised as though he needed to calm me.

Maybe he did. I'd been standing here all of a handful of seconds maybe. He hadn't walked past me. I knew it. I would have seen the movement out of the corners of my eye, at the very least.

And yet Vasco was right in front of me, as though he'd gone through the portal first.

Well, him and Magellan, who was standing next to Vasco, tail going like he was so very excited that we were finally here.

Magellan yipped happily.

"Give him a moment to adjust, Magellan," Vasco said. "Then he'll ask, I'm sure."

"Ask what?" I said, shaking my head. "I have so many questions I don't even know where to start anymore."

"Not much of a surprise. You've been through quite a bit today." Vasco chuckled. "Magellan here, though, he thinks your first question is how we got here ahead of you. And I admit, I'm tempted to address it first."

"Oh, let's," I said, with feeling.

"Simple. Every portal is different. Distinctive in some way. You wouldn't know that yet. No way that experiencing two is enough to get you going the right direction."

"Portal? What do you mean? I know 'portal' basically means 'door' but—"

"Very good," Vasco said, giving me a smile that Magellan supported with another happy bark. "But let's not get ahead of ourselves. You felt a ... slowing, didn't you? A sense that passing through was taking longer than it should have?"

"Oh, the last year or two of that step just seemed to fly by."

"Years. Heh. That's good. Watch for that if you go into Faerie."

"Faerie?"

"But for now," Vasco said quickly, one hand coming up again like I was a spooked horse, "let's stick to that portal you just walked through. The reason it felt so slow was that it was warded. Remember that. Warded portals feel slow. It's because the ward is assessing you and deciding whether or not to let you in."

I blinked at him. "Are you saying that the archway behind me" — I jerked my thumb, but did a double-take when I saw solid crystal where I'd expected an archway.

"Finish your question," Vasco said in a soothing tone. "It will make you feel better."

I tapped the solid crystal wall. Shook my head. Sighed. Turned back to Vasco.

Magellan barked encouragingly, and I remembered what I'd been in the middle of asking.

I almost lost another moment wondering if I'd just understood the bark of a dog, but shook my head and focused on the question I'd already started.

"The archway decided whether or not I got to walk through it?"

"Not the archway," Vasco said. "The portal. Specifically the wards we'd set up on the portal. Which was how Magellan and I got here before you, even though we entered after you. The wards know us, of course, so the portal whisked us right through."

I blinked at that. Tried to make sense of it. But I'd felt his presence behind me while my foot took that eternal journey through the ... though the portal.

That meant that there had to have been some point when I wasn't in that hallway, so Vasco and Magellan could enter without passing me. And yet, I couldn't have been through and in here yet, because they stepped in before I could.

"Breathe," Vasco said gently. "It helps to breathe. This is a lot to adjust to."

I nodded. Drew slow, deep breaths of the rose-scented air. Realized I could still hear the gentle strains of that Mozart sonata.

Wait. Had the music and the fragrance carried through that archway? Or did the same source reach both?

I almost asked about that, but Vasco had more to say.

"To continue, the archway was just an archway, just like the doorway to that Portland Loo was just a doorway. Until I activated the portal."

I frowned. "Where would the archway have led if you hadn't activated it?"

Magellan barked a five-set.

"Exactly, Magellan. He *is* quick." Vasco clapped me on the shoulder. "Nowhere. It would have led right into a wall of shale, deep inside Mount Hood."

"That hallway was inside Mount Hood?"

Mount Hood was miles from Portland. I didn't know how many — something like twenty or thirty, I thought — but I knew I could see it looking east from I5 while driving through town.

Just exactly how many times was my jaw going to drop today? If this kept up, my mom would get proven right. I would end up catching a fly. Or something worse.

Who knew just what those bats down here lived on?

I shook my head to clear the terrible image of little insects crying for help in perfect English.

And all the while Vasco nodded. Smiling. Waiting for the question he knew was coming.

"Then where are we now?"

"Now," Vasco said, sweeping one arm out wide to take in the whole of the crystal cavern. "Now we are in the very heart of Portal-land."

5

Vasco started walking again, Magellan beside him, nails clicking along the white crystal floor.

I hustled to catch up. I felt a chill, but I didn't think it was the cavern. Huge as it was, it seemed warm enough. I didn't even feel a draft, and I'd always figured anyplace this big had to be drafty.

Maybe it was nerves?

Just as I caught up to Vasco and Magellan, I saw where they were leading me. Stairs had been cut into the floor and the sides of the level below us.

In fact, now that I could get a little perspective, closer to the inner edge, it looked to me as though there were stairways down every place the color changed from one shade to the next.

The stairs even had handrails, cut out of the crystal walls of the stairwell, which were the same shade as the place they'd been cut in. In this case, between deep red and deep orange.

The smell of the air changed as we descended. No longer roses, but orange blossoms. The sound of the Mozart faded away too, and apart from our own passage down the stairs, the main thing I could hear was the echoes of some kind of argument from somewhere down below.

Magellan barked a complex nine-yip sequence, punctuated with a deeper woof.

"Probably why the place is so empty today," Vasco muttered, and I wasn't sure I was supposed to hear him.

"Why?" I asked.

"Oh, we'll get to that," he said, giving me a smile again. "We have so much more to cover before we reach the center of things."

"Great," I said, relief flooding my system. "Answers at last."

"Well," Vasco said as his smile veered toward mischief. "Let's be honest. They'll probably just lead to more questions. But that's good. The only time the questions really end is in death."

Magellan yipped something that sounded bureaucratic.

I know. But I swear that's how it sounded.

Vasco chuckled. "Magellan said that, before death, questions are the only thing more certain than taxes."

We were walking across the first level down now, and I saw that my guess was right. The direction of the wall colors reversed itself, compared to the pattern established above. Otherwise, this level seemed to be empty, apart from solid-looking, black metal doors set into the crystal walls every so often. I was pretty sure the doors were set in the center of each pattern.

"Let's start with Portal-land," Vasco said, distracting me from those doors. "Throughout the world, there are places where reality runs a bit ... thin."

"Thin," I said, tone flat.

"Think of our universe as a ... a leather ball. Now imagine that there are spots where the leather wears thing. Perhaps because of us on this side, or others on the other side, or possibly just through the passage of time."

"Or maybe design flaws?" I asked.

Magellan barked.

"He agrees with you, of course. I myself do not consider them flaws, but features. Then again, I also don't think the universe was designed, per se. Perhaps over time, you will come to see things my way."

"All right, so a portal is one of these spots where reality is thin?"

"Don't get ahead," Vasco said, shaking a finger at me, "or this will take all day."

I nodded, chastened.

"Now, these spots where reality is thin, some of them actually wear through. Those are naturally occurring portals. They're present twenty-four-seven. Sometimes they're unidirectional, sometimes they're bidirectional, but they're always open."

Magellan barked something that sounded argumentative.

"He's right, of course," Vasco said, nodding at Magellan. "Some of them do get closed and locked, but only by actions taken on this side or the other. And even then," — Vasco turned slightly to address the rest of this to his attentive beagle — "those seals and locks are tenuous at best. Very difficult to keep closed that which nature wishes open. Like trying to hold back the tides."

I drew breath to ask a question, but Vasco turned to me with one gray eyebrow high and I let my mouth closed.

He nodded. His wild hair bounced.

"Most countries have one or two of these natural portals. Usually somewhere out of the way, because most people naturally turn away from such things."

"The otter," I said. I couldn't help myself.

"Very good," Vasco said, nodding appreciatively while Magellan barked agreement. "You're right. Everyone near you heard that cry for help. But because it came from nonhuman lips, most humans selectively ignored it, the way they selectively ignore the sounds of planes flying overhead, or the casual rush of a breeze."

"But why did I hear it?"

"That is the key, isn't it?" Vasco chuckled again, as it seemed he had to every time he heard the word *key*. "You heard it and acknowledged that you heard it. You even responded. Put yourself at risk where another would have seen something too fantastical to believe. Closed his mind to what his eyes were showing him."

"But you had to have heard the otter." I frowned.

"I did. It woke me up." Vasco ducked his head, a bit chagrined himself for a change. "I was in deep sleep. I don't quite rouse as fast as I used to. By the time I reached the area, you had already handled the matter. And, alas, my arrival was ... not quite so timely as I might have wished. I was too late to spare you falling into the Willamette."

"So why did I hear the otter?"

"That's not for me to say," Vasco said. "To return to the subject."

I gnashed my teeth then, but I didn't interrupt as we crossed another, lower level, accompanied by the smell of sunflowers. This level had furniture here and there. All of it crystal, done in jewel tones, and looked to be set up for meeting areas and relaxation areas.

Again the color pattern of the walls reversed itself on this level, and the next set of stairs down awaited us at the junction between yellow and green. Pale shades, each.

And still those iron doors set into the walls, in the center of each color.

"Some places," Vasco continued. "Have several natural portals. The British Isles. Iceland. Egypt. India."

Magellan barked.

"You're right," Vasco said, "he doesn't need a full list here and now. The point is, portals occur more in some places than in others. No one can say exactly why. Here in the United States, Boston has a few nearby, as do Rhode Island, New Orleans, and a few other cities."

"Portland?" I prompted.

"Yes, well." Vasco gave me a proud smile. "Portland is the only city founded here *because* of its portals."

"But I thought—"

"Yes," Vasco said, cutting me off. "I know all about the common history of the area. Francis Pettygrove and Asa Lovejoy supposedly flipping a coin over who got to name the growing township after his hometown." Vasco shook his head. "Nonsense. Pettygrove's wife Sophia was the real power player there. And she was also a witch, who recognized the true potential of the region with the most natural portals in the western hemisphere."

"Sophia Pettygrove was a witch?"

"Still is. Or was, the last time I saw her," Vasco said with a smile.

"And she made sure historians got the story of that "hometown" nonsense to cover the truth. This was the Land of Portals. Portal-land. Or Portland, for short."

Magellan barked something that sounded like a joke I couldn't quite hear...

"Yes," Vasco said, chuckling. He frowned at me. "The jest doesn't translate well, I'm afraid. Dog humor is tied up in smells, and the closest I can come to giving you the spirit of what he just said is this."

Vasco cleared his throat.

"Calling it Portal-land on a map would smell like a kitchen where the fish get cleaned."

My turn to frown. I barely took in the change of furniture on the next level or the scent of fir trees as we continued to the next stairwell.

Magellan barked a correction. The smell of fish. The side effects.

"I'm trying," Vasco said. "It's kind of a way of saying that it would draw—"

Suddenly I got it. The barks I heard made sense to me. I'm not sure I can explain it in English any better than I did right then, but my impression burst out of me.

"It would draw every cat in the neighborhood, and make things hard on the dogs protecting the place."

It's not actually an anti-cat joke. Not the way Magellan told it, anyway. It was just about ... too much to handle.

I was chuckling anyway, while Magellan barked happily and Vasco nodded sagely.

"So," Vasco asked as we crossed the next floor, accompanied by the scent of bluebells. "Do you always understand Doggerel?"

I stopped walking and blinked at Vasco.

"There's no official name for the language of dogs," he said, looking back at me but still walking, "and if you have a better term for it, I'd like to hear it."

I hustled to catch up.

"Doggerel it is," I said. "And not that I know of. I've lived around cats most of my life. Always had a good rapport with them though."

Magellan barked something that sounded forgiving, though Vasco didn't translate it.

"Anyway," Vasco said as we descended the next staircase. "Sophia Pettygrove believed that the influx of settlers to the region would inevitably cause issues with the portals, either through accidental stumbling or ... malicious intent on the part of some of those who could recognize them for what they were."

"What about the natives?" I asked.

Vasco gave me another nod of approval while Magellan barked something similar. We were crossing another level down now, where the scent was one I didn't recognize. Subtle and sweet and herbal.

"The Multnomah were the major tribe in the area," Vasco said, "but they mostly avoided the portals the way most people do throughout the world."

"Mostly?"

"Just so. Those who felt drawn to the portals formed their own small tribe. The Kenocha." Vasco frowned. "We see them from time to time. Largely, though, they travel the portals and live among many different lands."

I thought about that for a few steps, and realized I could pick out some of the actual words of the argument below us, though the echoes of the huge crystal cavern.

"I don't care *what* he told you, we're not doing things that way."

Sure, that *sounded* like a young woman. But the otter had sounded like a young woman too. Maybe my mind just translated things that way?

I was ready to believe that about myself, so I tried not to draw conclusions about who was having that argument.

I do know that whoever she was arguing with had a high, squeaky voice. And that person wasn't speaking anything like English. Its words came out some kind of scree-ing hissing sound.

Then we reached the last staircase. And I knew it was the last staircase because I could see a whole floor ahead of me. Softly glowing white crystal just like every other floor.

Finally, some furniture that wasn't crystal.

In the center, a gigantic round table made from some dark, dark wood. This thing was huge. Way too big to be practical. Had to be a good hundred feet across.

Surrounding the table were scores of executive roller chairs and ... well, other things to sit on? In? Perching bars, fish tanks, and a weird variety of other options that didn't all make sense at once.

Off to the sides, away from the round table, were more of the styles of crystal furniture I'd seen above. Comfortable sitting areas around what looked like raised fire pits.

And there, to our left, the argument.

A girl in a wheelchair. On the heavy side. Teenager, from the look of her. Dark wavy hair made her skin look even paler than it might have on its own. Big black-rimmed glasses.

She was leaning forward and shoving a finger in the face of the...

"What the fuck?"

What can I say? The words leapt out of my mouth before I could think.

Up above, I'd mentioned all those flying bats? Yellow fur, black wings, all that?

Well, she was arguing with one of those bats. Except that this one was standing on its back legs. And it stood at least eight feet tall.

My cry of surprise interrupted the argument. The girl and the giant bat both turned to check out the interlopers.

"That's him!" the giant bat screeched, pointing with a long, long wing. "That's the one!"

"Now calm down," the girl said.

"No!" the bat screeched. "He must die!"

6

A BUNCH OF THINGS HAPPENED AT ONCE.

The giant bat creature leaped into the air. Wings flapping. It screeched something not even close to English.

All those bats flying up above? Out of the corner of my eye I could see them start to dive.

All of them.

The girl in the wheelchair started shouting.

Vasco leapt in front of me, shouting just as loud.

Magellan started running circles on the white crystal floor, barking.

The sounds all became white noise, lost in the echoes of this enormous, prismatic crystal chamber.

I had to do something. And I didn't have my thermos to throw.

The stairwell wouldn't protect me. It was wide enough for the big bat creature, let alone the smaller bats.

No ceilings anywhere under the—

Childhood earthquake training kicked in.

I bolted for the giant table. Yeah, it was a good full-court away, and it looked heavy enough to flatten a semi, but it had more legs than a centipede.

I figured it might hold.

Long freaking sprint, but I was still riding high and strong from that key lime gumball. Felt like I could have left LeBron himself in my rearview.

Unfortunately, the bat creature was faster than LeBron.

Claws raked my shoulder. Tore off my shirt. Fiery pain lanced right down my back.

I dove. Rolled. Scrambled past a roller chair that went teetering out across the crystal floor. Clawed my way across that glowing white floor. Aiming for the center of the table.

The big bat creature landed. Ducked and looked under the table at me. Screeched frustration. Knocked chairs aside.

Smaller bats landed now. Started crawling across the floor toward me, chirping something as they came. Their big brown eyes all promised pain. Maybe death.

They weren't exactly small, either. Big as good-sized dogs, those things.

Suddenly the girl's voice boomed out louder than all the other sounds in the room.

"I said no!"

Another word followed that no. I was sure of it. I heard it. I knew I did. But the instant she finished the word, it fled from my mind. Like a dream that had seemed intensely real until the alarm went off, then even the subject of the dream fled, let alone the details.

The word was kind of like that. I knew I heard it. Until I didn't hear it anymore. Then it was a faint idea just outside my mental grasp.

But the not-word had its effect.

Every one of those bats — giant bat creature included — fell to the ground.

Not dead. Not even unconscious. In fact, the giant bat creature immediately rolled over and looking in the direction of the girl in the wheelchair.

All the smaller bats stayed where they were. They were looking at me, but the promise of pain was gone from their eyes.

Honestly, they looked cute and fuzzy again. Like they'd never been little flying death machines.

Still. I didn't trust it. I was bleeding from the shoulder and upper back, and the pain was still intense enough that I had to grit my teeth.

"You can come out." The girl's voice, soothing. "They won't harm you now." Her voice got harder. "*Will* you, Chiron?"

The giant bat creature drummed its wing fingers on the crystal floor in a disturbing little sound.

"No," it said, it's voice high and still a little too close to a screech for my comfort. "I and mine shall delay our vengeance."

Chiron turned its eyes toward me. "At the *insistence* of the Lady of the Portals."

I just sat there for a moment, hissing my breaths against the pain. It might have been my imagination, but I would have sworn that the burning sensation was spreading down my spine.

Magellan trotted up to me. Barked a four-piece that felt strangely reassuring.

"Honestly," the girl — the Lady of Portals, I supposed — said reassuringly. "You can come out now..."

"Scott," Vasco said.

"You can come out now, Scott. At the very least, you'll want me to look at your wound."

"Don't let the pain reach your waist," Vasco said. "It'll go badly for you if it does."

Magellan trotted a few steps away. Stopped. Looked back and barked. Then repeated the movement.

Using one hand and both feet — my left shoulder objected to taking my weight — I made my way after the beagle. Which, fortunately, didn't lead me near any of the bats. Especially not Chiron.

Before I reached the edge I could see that Magellan was leading me to the Lady of Portals.

Hissing in a deep breath — the pain was to the bottom of my rib cage now — I pushed aside one more roller chair and stood up.

"My," the Lady of Portals said, looking me up and down. "Hello, salty goodness." She turned her head. "Vasco. It's not even my birthday."

"Uh…" I started, but she laughed.

Her laugh had a nerdy, dorky kind of charm that was infectious. I found myself laughing too, despite the pain.

"She's teasing," Vasco clarified, approaching, while Chiron called over the smaller bats and began … well, I'd call it muttering, but it was more like a muted version of their screeching.

"Turn and crouch down," the Lady of Portals said.

I did as she bid, and she said a few more words that fled my memory the moment she said them. She began rubbing the area of my wound with hands that glowed the pale green of mint chip ice cream. Suited the scent coming from those hands.

Cool relief spread right through me. My muscles relaxed so quickly I felt a buzzing in my head. My breaths got deeper, and the whole cavern brightened.

She kept going, careful to get the whole of the slash. Must have gotten more of me than I thought…

"I believe you've covered the wound, Janna," Vasco said, one eyebrow high. "And then some."

"Oh, all right," the Lady of Portals — Janna — said, and stopped rubbing. "You can be such a killjoy, Vasco. You should feel those shoulders."

She leaned in closer. Her voice quieter. "I don't suppose Chiron got your chest at all? Abs maybe?"

"No," I said, standing and turning around. "Just the shoulder."

Vasco pulled a tee shirt out of his duffel bag, and handed it to me.

"Pity," Janna said as I put on the tee shirt.

Then I frowned, because it looked exactly like the shirt Chiron had just torn off me, right down the U.C. Monterey logo. Even had the aftermath of a small blood stain near the collar from the time I got hacked on a layup by a guy who really needed to cut his fingernails.

"We are leaving," Chiron announced.

"No," Janna said, her voice suddenly icy with authority. The room seemed to still as she finished her statement. "You're not going anywhere. Not if you want to come through to this world again in my lifetime."

"You would—"

"You have a complaint," she said, rolling her chair between me and Chiron. "You will make it. He will answer it. Then I will rule. Do you agree?"

Chiron pulled in his wings. His wing fingers drummed on his fur.

Vasco set down his duffel bag. Stepped beside Janna, between me and Chiron. Took up what looked like a defensive stance.

Magellan took up position on Janna's other side. His head low, jaws apart. A faint growl issued from him.

The other bats gathered around Chiron. Chirping challenges of their own.

Chiron then straightened and snapped his wings out wide.

"I have decided," he announced. "We shall stay, and I shall issue my complaint. Which, *properly*, is the complaint of the Va-a-naska."

That last word seemed to echo more through the chamber than any other sound. I started batting it around in my head.

Va. Vaaaah.

A. Ahhhh.

Naska. Naaah-skaaaah.

There was something familiar about it, but I couldn't say why.

"Very well," Janna said, and I thought she sounded displeased, but I was only paying half-attention because I was still batting that word around in my head. "State the case of the Va-a-naska."

"This one." Chiron pointed at me dramatically. "This human. Native to this world and these lands. This one, who has been called Scott. This one, who stands shoulder height to me, with hair like summer wildgrass, and skin like—"

"We have established that you are referring to Scott Angus Eagle-son," Janna said.

Did *everyone* know my middle name? I sure never used it. Made me sound like a reject from *Braveheart*. But apparently Dad had a favorite uncle Angus, who died in Viet Nam, so complaining would have sounded petty.

"Very well." Chiron pulled his wings in close to his body. "This Scott Angus Eagleson."

"I'm the only Scott present," I said. "Shall we just stick to that?"

Chiron leaned forward and chirped an objection. But then he straightened up.

"Very well, this one who chooses to be called Scott. He willingly and intentionally slew a *riskatan*, not two hours past. He did so when it posed no threat to him. He did so when it was in the act of lawful hunting."

"Wait," I said, stepping forward. "Is he talking about the fish monster?"

"He dismisses it," Chiron said, pointing again, "as humans dismiss all things they do not understand. And like so many humans before him, he slew the 'monster' without considering his actions."

"I saved a talking otter from being eaten."

"Ridiculous," Chiron said. The bats around him all chirped agreement. "He has not the smell of a Locksmith."

Janna held up a hand to stop me from responding. To Chiron she said, "Is your complaint complete, or have you more to add?"

"I have brought forth all the pertinent *facts*."

Chiron's bats chorused agreement.

Janna turned her chair.

"Scott," she said, her tone gentler. "Tell me in your own words what happened."

"Delays!" Chiron objected. "Needless delays. All pertinent facts—"

"I will hear his words," Janna said, without looking away from me.

Chiron chirped, and his bats began complaining until Janna raised a hand. Then they, too, fell silent.

"Go on, Scott."

"I'd just finished a game of basketball in Riverfront Park, when I heard what I thought was a woman call for help. I tried to get a couple of my teammates to come help me check it out. I figured three big guys will chase off a problem faster than one."

Chiron chirped and screeched an objection.

"Take to the air," Janna said, spinning in her wheelchair to face Chiron. "If you cannot listen quietly, spend your aggression through your wings. I will hear his story."

Chiron leaned forward and chirped at her. Some of his bats took to the air, but he remained, wings folded, brown eyes glaring at me.

I didn't embellish what happened. I explained about the otter, and the fish monster. The pleading for help. The thrown thermos. Even my unexpected dip.

Unless I was mistaken, the image of me falling into the river brought a sparkle to Janna's eyes. But if so, no smile ever approached her lips.

I finished with Officer Martinez helping me over the rail.

"There," Chiron said. "He admitted flinging the projectile with murderous intent. He—"

"Vasco," Janna said, talking over Chiron, who fell into sullen silence. "You were present in Riverfront Park, I believe. Did you hear a *dorach* cry for help?"

"I did hear a cry for help, pitch and timbre consistent with the voice of a *dorach*. The cry woke me up. I also heard the call repeated."

"Did you witness Scott's actions?"

"I saw him throw and fall. I did not see a *dorach* or any *riskatan*."

Magellan began barking.

Chiron chirped another complaint, but Janna's attention was on Magellan.

"Magellan supports Scott's version," she said, turning to Chiron, "and confirms having heard a *dorach* cry for help. Locksmith or not, Scott clearly acted in response to that cry for help. Which means he did, indeed, intentionally defend a *dorach* from being eaten by a *riskatan*."

"He *killed* it," Chiron said. "Does its nonhuman nature excuse his crime?"

"The *riskatan* had no right to hunt the waters of the Willamette. It should never have left the Columbia." Over Chiron's immediate objections, she continued, "Furthermore, the *riskatan* was not hunting an otter, but a *dorach*. Which is a pertinent fact you left out, I note."

"I have heard nothing of *dorachs* in the Willamette," Chiron said. "The story is farce. Vasco awoke from a dream, heard a sound, and leaped to the wrong conclusion. If this Scott heard anything, he clearly mistook it. As for Magellan, he could be lying out of loyalty."

"Nice try," Janna said. "But the presence of witnesses supports Scott's version. He was deliberately and intentionally protecting a *dorach* from murder and consumption against the Va-a-naska Treaty."

"That does not permit him to commit murder. But he is human, so you will forgive his actions. Is this so? Is this your justice, Lady of the Portals?"

"No," Janna said, and this time she sighed in a way that gave me a cold feeling in my stomach. "I freely confess I would *like* to give him a pass, because I believe the *riskatan's* death was accidental, because the *riskatan* shouldn't have been there in the first place, and because it should not have hunted a *dorach*. Not to mention that Scott is not a Locksmith and does not know the treaties."

She sighed again, and that cold feeling started spreading chills up my spine and down my legs.

"However, my own desires are moot. The fact is, Scott, you did kill the *riskatan*. I've seen the corpse. When you hit it with your thermos, you snapped its neck. Intentionally or not. And I can't let that go unpunished, or the entire treaty system falls apart."

SUDDENLY I FELT VASTNESS OF THAT GIANT CRYSTAL CHAMBER AROUND me. Chiron and his bats were still nearby. Janna, Vasco and Magellan, even closer.

And yet I stood there, feeling more alone than I'd felt since Katy left me. Almost numb from the realization of what I'd done.

One word just echoed in my head.

"Killed."

I killed something. Or maybe I should say, I killed some*one*.

The fish monster. The *riskatan*. I killed it.

Me. The guy who didn't even kill spiders in his apartment. Flies and mosquitoes, sure. Ants, of course. But spiders got escorted outside. Used to drive Katy crazy. Made her call me Gandhi.

And yet I killed something today.

No.

Not some*thing*.

Some*one*.

Regret washed over me, as icy and shocking as the waters of the Willamette.

I dropped backwards into a sitting position, not caring how hard my butt hit that white crystal floor.

I fell backward with a little more care, so I didn't knock myself out.

I lay there. Gazing up at that huge black circle where the rainbow colors of the domed ceiling came together. From this position I could see that the rainbow pattern of each level rotated slowly — oh, so very slowly — each floor the opposite direction of the floor above it.

Apparently, Janna's pronouncement of doom had been enough for Chiron. He and his bats took to the air.

With only a portion of my attention, I watched them fly an arrow formation straight at a spot in the middle of the violet portion of the upper cavern walls.

They chirped before hitting, and each of them just vanished instead of splatting against the wall.

Normally, that might have fascinated me. Might have made me wonder if each color section in this vast chamber was actually a portal.

Right then, though, I noted their movement only cursorily. Most of my mind focused down on that one fact.

Murder.

I had committed murder.

I had done the most heinous thing one living person could do to another.

Maybe they should have let Chiron kill me.

Worst of all, I didn't even know the *riskatan's* name. Or anything about it. I knew I had murdered another being, but I had no sense of the true scope of what I had done.

Magellan interrupted my chain of thoughts. He trotted up and licked my face.

I looked over into the forgiving eyes of the beagle.

"I murdered someone, Magellan," I said. "I can't believe it. I'm a murderer."

Magellan made a small, whining sound of denial.

I looked over at Janna. I needed to know just how much damage I'd done today. Janna, though, was in quiet conversation with Vasco. They were at least a dozen feet away from me now.

When had they moved away?

Louder, to Janna, I said, "Did the *riskatan* have children?"

She didn't hear me. Her wheelchair was facing away, and Vasco was leaning in for their hushed argument.

I cleared my throat. Started to ask again.

Magellan didn't let me. He spun a circle. Ran over to Janna and Vasco, and ran circles around them, barking. His little tail going like mad the entire time.

I would have sworn that he was taking them to task about something.

"Oh!" Vasco said suddenly. He turned to me with an astonished expression, then back to Janna. "He thinks—"

"On it," Janna said, rolling her wheelchair over to me.

"You misunderstand," Janna said quickly. "*Riskatani* are not, properly speaking, sapient. They are sentient, more or less, but they're not intelligent, thinking individuals."

"But—"

"Their cunning can ape intelligence in a number of ways. Which makes them close enough that the Va-a-naska insisted that they be included in their treaty. And against my predecessor's better judgment, she agreed."

"Wait," I said, sitting up. Puzzled now. "Am I a murderer or am I not?"

"Well," Janna said, drawing the word out while Vasco crouched down and scratched Magellan up and down his back.

"No," Vasco said. "In every sense of the word that *matters*, you are not a murderer. You *saved* lives today."

"*Technically*," Janna said to me over whatever Vasco would have said next, "you *are* a murderer. But only because of the wording of the treaty, not the way you think of murder. *Riskatani* form no societies. They do not pair bond, nor raise their hatchlings. They do not fashion or wield tools. They show no more interest in their dead than they do any hunk of edible meat. They keep no histories. They can form packs for a time, but even those packs dissolve shortly or they end up killing each other because their nature is vicious and brutal."

"We don't restrain their hunting grounds with words," Vasco added. "There are magics that keep them out of the places they aren't supposed to go. It's the only way."

"They sound like monsters," I said.

"They are," Vasco said. "In pretty much every sense of the word. And I've long argued for their exclusion from the treaties."

"Which we won't get," Janna responded, sounding as though this were an old discussion she didn't want to get into again. "Not unless we give the Va-a-naska concessions that we're unwilling to make. They know the position this puts us in."

"That *ristakan* was in the Willamette, and we didn't know," Vasco said firmly. "If Scott hadn't killed it, it might have gotten not just that *dorach*, but a human swimmer. Possibly a child. Possibly more than one."

"And yet," Janna said, in a tone that said the discussion was over, "if I don't punish Scott for his actions, I violate the treaty. It's unfair, but we can thank my predecessor for that."

"What if—" Vasco started, but Janna cut him off with a wave of her hand. She turned to me. Rolled right up to me.

"I *must* punish you, Scott." Suddenly her brown eyes seemed to carry the weight of decades. Centuries maybe. "Chiron thinks you must die, but he is mistaken. You did what you did because a *dorach* requested aid. Even the death of the *riskatan* was accidental."

"I didn't know," I said, frustrated now. "I've never even heard of these things before. *Riskatan. Dorach.* Va-a-naska. I don't even—"

"Exactly," Janna said. "You acted out of ignorance. So, I give you a choice."

She lifted one hand. "You can *choose* ignorance. If you do, I will close your mind to the ... unusual portions of today's events, as well as your ability to notice the unusual. Basically, I would remove from you the essence of a Locksmith."

"No!" Vasco cried, while Magellan barked ardent agreement with his master. "To waste such talent would—"

"Be *his* choice," Janna said, her eyes never leaving me. "*If* that's what he chooses."

"What would I lose with my ... essence? This doesn't sound good."

"It *isn't* good," Vasco grumbled.

"Not *your* essence," Janna clarified, "but your Locksmith's essence. You would lose the ability to hear the speech of a *dorach*. To notice the little ways in which the world is not what most humans might expect it to be. You would become, well, normal."

"What's my other option?" I asked.

"That *riskatan* should never have been in the Willamette. I do not believe that it traveled there of its own. It would not risk the restraints keeping it from populated areas without a pack to goad it on. But no signs of a pack have been seen."

"Which means..." I said.

"Which means that someone deliberately set a *riskatan* loose in the Willamette. Perhaps as a distraction. Perhaps as part of some larger plot. Either way..."

Janna lifted her other hand. "If you choose knowledge, your punishment is to be the one who investigates this. Make no mistake, this will likely be dangerous."

"How could I possibly—"

"It would mean," Janna said, and now that sparkle was back in her eye, "that you would have to be trained as a Locksmith of the Portals. You would be taught of the peoples and creatures you would be likely to meet, as well as the alliances such as the Va-a-naska. You would learn the magic of portals, their uses, their pathways and so forth. Along with a few other ... related skills."

"You'd have to learn to fight, too," Vasco added, standing straighter as though to show off the muscles he still had, despite all that gray hair. "Properly fight. So you could have stood against Chiron if you had to. A Locksmith must be able to defend himself."

"You certainly have the tools on that front," Janna said, looking me up and down again.

She shook her head and cleared her throat.

"Excuse me. Scott Angus Eagleson, this is my judgment as current Lady of the Portals. You acted out of ignorance, so you may choose ignorance. You killed a *riskatan* that should not have been where it was, doing what it did. So if you choose knowledge, you must be the one to resolve that mystery, wherever it leads."

Wherever it leads. That sounded kind of open-ended and danger- ous. No doubt there were even scarier things waiting for me than Chiron and his bats.

Not that ignorance sounded like a much better option. I could still see those people in Riverfront Park, turning and walking away from the *dorach's* cries for help. Not even consciously hearing those cries.

If I had turned away too, maybe Vasco could have responded in time to save the *dorach*...

Or maybe the *dorach* would be dead. And maybe that *riskatan* would be feasting on children right now.

Plus, whoever loosed that *riskatan*, they might do something even worse.

I sucked in a deep breath and spat it out.

"I choose knowledge. When do I start?"

8

I'M NOT SURE WHAT I WAS EXPECTING. MAYBE THAT TRAINING TO BE A Locksmith of the Portals would be like college, and I'd join some kind of series of lectures about treaties, and workshops about portals. Maybe become one of many students.

Like maybe there was some kind of Hogwarts lurking under Portland.

Or maybe it would be like a martial arts class, or...

That wasn't how things worked.

When I agreed to choose knowledge for my punishment instead of ignorance, Janna thanked me, but then turned and wheeled away right through a red, glowing hole in the air that hadn't been there the moment before and spiraled down into nothingness as soon as she was through it.

"Did you see it?" Vasco asked quickly, his voice low and urgent.

"The portal? Yeah. Of course."

"No," Vasco said, shaking his head so that his wild gray hair shook. "Did you see what happened to the portal?"

"It spiraled down—"

"After." Vasco stepped in close. His musky, animal-like scent mixed oddly with the undercurrent of violets in the air. "What happened after it spiraled down?"

I shook my head.

"First lesson. Miss nothing."

"How can I—"

"Perception is a matter of attention. You must learn to stretch your awareness."

"How?"

Vasco smiled.

He spread his arms and dropped a portal on me.

The portal was orange, and smelled vaguely of cinnamon. As it passed over me — or I through it — I could hear a faint crackling, like a Jacob's Ladder.

I noticed all that as a sideline, though. Most of me was thinking that this was grossly unfair. How could he just drop a portal on me? Weren't portals a thing you had to choose to pass through?

Yes and no. That was lesson two, I suppose. Although I was now entirely inside lesson one.

Passing though that portal felt like falling in all directions at once. My poor stomach didn't know what to make of that, and my inner ear was mostly trying to tell me I'd lost my friggin' mind.

But I wasn't falling. I wasn't even leaning.

No. I was flat on my feet. Standing in a hallway full of mirrors.

Notice everything, Vasco'd said.

Well the first thing I noticed was that while the portal smelled like cinnamon, the hallway full of mirrors smelled like polished silver. Freshly polished silver, with hints of that polish still lingering in the air, along with the dust motes.

The hallway itself stretched out in two directions, as far as I could see. I wasn't sure how far that was though. Where I stood was lit up brightly, with a yellowish sort of light. But I could tell that shifted no more than a few hundred feet each direction.

And beyond that, I could see areas of blackness.

And then there were the mirrors themselves.

They seemed to come in all sizes and shapes, from tiny little ones that might have fit on the blade of a comb to great big ones that stretched from the reddish carpeting to the ceiling, some fifteen feet up.

Some of the mirrors were framed, and others just bare. Some of them were mounted on the same kind of tan stucco as I'd seen in that passageway inside Mount Hood. Others seemed to be mounted on larger mirrors.

The two nearest me were both round. An oval in front of me and a round mirror behind me. Both about the same size. Like I could have stretched one arm across them, but only just.

The mirrors reflected me. But they didn't reflect each other.

No. It seemed that each mirror seemed to reflect me standing somewhere else.

The oval one in front of me, it showed me standing on the edge of the basketball courts at Riverfront Park. Only one game going now, and none of my teammates still there.

Just how long had I been gone?

I'd lost all sense of time, once I'd stepped through the — *details, Scott* — green portal in the doorway of the Portland Loo.

I stopped. Blinked at myself. Noticed the sky — still light, but the streetlights were clicking on all the same.

No. That wasn't possible. I couldn't have been gone that long.

I turned around.

The round mirror reflected the same scene. Except my teammates were there. Jolly was talking to Shorty. And there was Metallica greeting Red...

Greeting?

The sky was bright blue up above. And that park was more crowded than it was in the mirror behind me.

I spun. Yep. Clearly late afternoon there, verging onto early evening.

I spun back. Definitely morning. Before I arrived, because I hadn't been there when Red greeted Metallica with a hug, like an old friend. I'd thought they'd met today, same as me.

Unless this wasn't *this* morning I was looking at...

Could it be tomorrow?

Was I looking at the same scene in different times?

I shook myself. Swallowed hard against the rising lump in My throat.

My heart started pounding.

Of all the things I'd seen so far, this ... this felt the most fantastic.

Could portals carrying me through time?

If so, could I go back and save the *dorach* without killing the *riskatan*?

"Hello?" I called out. "Do I get to ask questions?"

My voice echoed out, returning my own words to me, over and over, until they faded away.

"I guess that's a no," I mumbled. But even my soft words echoed back at me twice before fading away entirely.

I picked a direction and started walking.

Every mirror reflected me, but otherwise showed me an entirely different scene.

Some I recognized, like the weird statue just outside Powell's Books downtown. It was a huge thing, made of brushed steel. It looked to me like a giant whisk set into a tripod, so that passersby could push the round end and the bristles would move back and forth, up above.

Another scene was the stag statue, down closer to the river. The stag sat in the middle of a street, on a tiny island of its own.

Other scenes showed ferns and Douglas firs. One showed a dock that looked old and cold. A seaport, not a riverport.

Castles and country sides, islands and forests, mountain peaks and snow-ridden caves. The Colosseum in Rome. The Great Sphinx in Egypt.

That one I had to stop and stare at for a moment, whirling back and forth between the huge rectangle mirrors on either side of me. Both showed the sphinx.

But on my left, the sphinx's nose was whole, and its face unravaged by time.

After that, the scenes got even stranger.

Dark underground tunnels. Sleek interiors that looked for all the world to me as though they belonged on spaceships.

One, I swear, was on an asteroid.

And then, there were the people.

At the start, they were all humans.

But when I got to the Eiffel Tower, I noticed that there were a handful of tourists that looked, well...

They stood a head taller than anyone else around them, and they looked too skinny to be healthy. Their skins were all the shade of oak bark in summer, and they were stark naked.

But that nudity, it didn't look nude. They didn't have, well, genitals. At least, not any kind I could recognize.

Their eyes slanted vertically instead of horizontally, but their eyelids still flapped the same direction that human eyelids do. And their eyes had no pupils. They were all shades of color that looked like leaves. Greens and yellows and reds.

No humans around them were paying them any mind. The humans gave them a wide berth without seeming to notice them at all. These tree people just wandered as they chose, gazing up at the Eiffel Tower like they were just any other kinds of tourists.

And the tree people weren't the only nonhuman things I saw.

Countless varieties, from the kinds I'd seen depicted in films and TV shows to types I couldn't begin to guess at.

Creatures of air, and others of fire. Creatures that looked to be made of pure electricity. Werewolves. Snake creatures, and entities that appeared to be composed of trails of black smoke.

Even tiny gnomes in red hats, and great big orcs.

Yes. Orcs. Green skins, small tusks, the whole nine. Just like the elves I saw were beautiful, with hair that looked to have been spun from precious metals, and the kind of skin that models would envy.

I couldn't keep track of it all. I just found myself hoping there wouldn't be a test later. There was no way I could remember or describe every setting, every creature, all the wonders I saw.

But of them all, there was one wonder that stood tall and proud above the others.

It was a junction of nine rainbows in the sky.

No. Not in one sky. In nine skies that came together. The skies around each rainbow held their color starkest near their own rainbow, fading to the next sky as they approached the other rainbows.

Some skies were dark blue and purples, others were pale blues and greens, one was orange, and one was a bright, vivid red. Crimson, maybe. Colors were never my strength.

But the place they all came together, that spot was blacker than midnight. The kind of black that made me think of the void of deep space.

I stopped there. Two mirrors in that spot in the hall. Both round, and maybe eight feet across.

And both reflected exactly the same scene.

I hadn't seen all the mirrors. Not by any stretch. The farther I walked, the farther the hallway seemed to stretch. And I knew it never looped on itself — not so far, at least — because I'd never seen the same mirrors.

Still, from what I had seen, this was the only spot in the hallway where both mirrors reflected the same thing.

And what they reflected, it put me in mind of the crystal cavern. Only there, instead of nine rainbows, they had the seven colors *of* the rainbow, climbing the walls until they met in a circle just as black as that spot where the rainbows joined here.

Details, Scott. What else do you notice?

I started laughing then. The scent. It was faint. Only just barely noticeable. But it was the smell of violets.

This was the only spot that had smelled of violets. I'd arrived through cinnamon and landed in the odor of polished silver. An odor that had faded in places and grew strong in others, and yet it was always present.

Now that I thought about it, I could smell polished silver here too. Like an overlay above the fragrance of the violets.

But the scent of violets was definitely there.

Violets. The bottom chamber of the crystal cavern smelled like violets.

"Is that it?" I called out. "Is that the secret?"

My own words came back to me, getting softer and softer.

Is that it? Is that the secret?

Is that it? Is that the secret?

Is that it? Is that the secret?

Is that...

No answers were coming. This was either a trap or a puzzle. I had to find my own way out.

And this looked like as good a place as any.

I looked left. Then right. Flared my nostrils in a deep breath, making sure I really did smell those violets.

I turned right and jumped into the mirror.

9
_____

"Aaaaaaaaaaaaaaaaaaaaaaaaaaaaah!"

I'm not sure how long I was falling through blackness when I started yelling.

All right. I was screaming.

I was falling rapidly through a shaft of pure blackness. I couldn't even see my own hands, my nose, anything.

I could feel wind resistance, chapping my lips and rippling my cheeks and skin. My hair must have been flying wild as Vasco's, if not as gray nor as long.

The air was cold. It felt chilly all the way to my lungs. And smelled like it was full of water vapor. I didn't know if that was good or bad.

Frankly, though, it wasn't the air I was worried about. It was the ground.

Presuming that I wasn't going to be falling forever — and that I'd been falling long enough to get past the screaming and on to actually thinking about my situation meant that maybe I _would_ be falling forever — but if I didn't, sooner or later I was going to hit the ground.

And I'd long ago reached terminal velocity. So when my poor

body eventually slammed into the ground, I'd probably leave a splatter zone that could be measure in kilometers.

The pain was likely to go beyond anything I could imagine. Still, I did have the consolation that I wouldn't feel it very long. I'd be pulp. Or a puddle.

Or maybe I was in space and I'd burn up on...

No. I couldn't have been in space. There was wind resistance. The vacuum of space might not have been perfect, but it wouldn't have given me wind resistance.

Also, actual space would have frozen me. I didn't know that from experience, of course, but I couldn't believe that *all* of my science fiction had lied to me.

Still, I wasn't freezing. A little chilly, maybe, but not freezing.

I could breathe, too. Which meant I couldn't have been all that high up, cosmically speaking. I mean, I'd read about special forces guys doing those high-altitude, low-opening jumps. HALO, they called them. They started at high enough altitudes that they needed oxygen just to avoid passing out, because the air was too thin to breathe.

I was breathing, but I wasn't passing out. So I couldn't have been starting as high as they did.

I couldn't decide if that was a consolation. After all, I had no reason to believe I was falling towards the earth.

Some of the images I'd seen in mirrors had been out in space. And others, maybe entirely different planes of existence.

That line of thought didn't help. In fact, I'd just reached the point of trying to scream again — just to see if it made me feel better — when my eyes finally detected a change in my environment.

Light.

I could see light.

Faint light, but white and straight ahead of me.

The light slowly grew stronger.

It began to spread out. Not in the way dawn rose, with a general lightening in the environment.

No, it began to spread out in two lines. Like a giant X. And at the center of the X, a yellow spot.

The light itself was so white it was almost blue, the way fluorescent lights could get. But in the middle, a warmer yellow spot. Like an area of incandescence in the center of all that fluorescence.

But the lines of that X were cut tight. As though the blackness allowed only so much light, and was determined to contain it within its specified zone.

I found myself wishing I'd tried skydiving. Maybe I could have controlled my fall. Slowed myself. Picked my landing spot.

Landing. Hah.

I did do what little I could think of to slow myself down. I forced my body to turn so that the wind resistance was hitting all of me at once, instead of just my face.

Didn't help much. Now *all* of my skin was getting rippled, even what was covered by my shorts, shoes and tee shirt.

I tried not to think about that. Just focused on the yellow circle in the center of the outstretched arms of the giant X.

I found myself grateful that my stomach wasn't nearly as full as it felt. I'd only had the one little restorative treat, and its key lime taste was still faint on my tongue.

The yellow zone grew larger and larger. I was getting closer and closer.

I could see more of that yellow zone now. It glistened. As though it were all yellow crystal.

So much for my vague hopes of a soft landing. Maybe a bunch of angels — or maybe giant eagles or something — catching me and lowering me gently to the ground.

If anything, I seemed to start falling faster. That was impossible, though. That...

I stopped that line of thought right there. As many impossible things as I'd seen today?

So, I was falling faster and faster as I got closer and closer to that yellow crystal zone in the middle of the giant X.

I shook my head. Closed my eyes. Began uttering prayers to a God I wasn't sure I really believed in in the first place.

I hit that yellow crystal floor at full speed...

...and bounced.

I sank down into the floor as though it were made of rubber, and sprang right back out into the blackness.

I'm pretty sure I yelled a few expletives in there, out of sheer shock.

No idea how far back up I flew, but I came down hard enough to bounce a second time.

And then a third.

And then a fourth.

I think I must have bounced about sixteen times in all.

But on that last landing, suddenly, the floor wasn't rubbery at all anymore. It was all hard, yellow crystal.

But I was falling so slowly by this point that I could get my feet under me and land with what I'd like to think was catlike grace.

I threw my hands in the air and yelled out, "Ta-daaaaa!"

Someone snickered.

I looked around.

The area nearest me all looked to be crystal flooring the color of ripe lemons, with a soft glow the same shade coming out of it.

Starting about thirty feet from me, though, crystals jabbed up through the smooth floor. Thick, they were, varying between one foot and three feet wide. Some of them came up only as high as my knee, others went up taller and taller until they seemed to form a crystal forest around me. Complete with branches coming off of them, and tiny crystal maple leaves.

From the clearing where I stood, I couldn't see far enough through the crystal forest to tell where those channels were, that would have formed the branches of the giant X.

However, just between two of the nearer crystal trees, I could see a person.

Not a human, mind you. A person. And as of today, that was a distinction that I needed to keep in mind.

Humans were people, but they were clearly not the only people around.

This person was short. Maybe three, three-and-a-half feet tall. And he had a long, hooked beak. Kind of like a vulture. Under robes of yellow-orange, he or she looked to have more-or-less humanoid construction.

I mean, this person seemed to be standing on feet. Yes, those feet had dark purple talons, but they still wore worn leather sandals.

And those feet appeared to be at the end of legs, at least so far as I could tell under the thick robes.

This person had arms, too, coming out of the robe. Dark purple talon-like hands as well, clutching what I thought was a gnarled oaken staff.

A hood was drawn up over the back of this person's head, but not far enough to obscure his or her facial features.

Big, oval eyes, taller than they were wide. With pupils that would have looked more at home on a lizard than a bird. Wizened cheeks of a rough, purple color, that went with the similar shades of the talons that I could see.

I caught myself starting to bow, and turned it into a half-bow. But that might not have been enough to be respectful, so I threw in an elaborate hand gesture, coming out from my head like a salute and trailing back until it looked more like I was bowing after all.

I stopped myself. Stood up straighter.

The bird-person tilted his or her head. Made this clucking, ticking sound. Not like a chicken, but more like the way a car engine ticks as it cools down. Especially on an older car.

"Um," I said into the uncomfortable silence. "Hello?"

Nothing.

"My name is Scott Eagleson. I think Vasco sent me?"

Still nothing. Maybe a blink.

"I'm not sure I'm supposed to be here though. I took a chance, jumping into a mirror and ... well ... here I am?"

The bird-person started snickering again.

Then the snicker got louder.

Finally I found myself flushing a bright red while the bird person was wheezing with laughter, clapping the tip of its staff on the ground as though trying to get hold of itself.

"Right," I said at last. "Clearly this is a mistake. Maybe the exit is down one of those branches."

I frowned. Looked at the bird-person. "I don't suppose you know the way back to the rainbow crystal cavern."

"Smell," the bird-person said, in a voice that could have been the muted cry of a hawk.

"The way back is—"

"Smell. The. Air." The bird-person smacked the tip of his or her staff on the crystal. "Now."

"Okay," I said quickly, my hands coming halfway up in surrender.

I sucked in a deep breath through my nostrils. Sure enough, there was a subtle scent to the air.

I was pretty sure the fragrance I could pick up was one I knew. Confirmation would help though.

"Honeysuckle?"

"Does that *sound* right to you? For this place?"

"How can a smell..." I frowned. Looked around at all the yellow-ish, slightly glowing crystal.

I shook my head.

"No. This place should have more of a ... yellowish scent. Lemons, maybe, if I had to guess by the shade of the crystal."

"Better," the bird-person said. Then nodded, once, sharply. "Why doesn't it fit?"

"Well, honeysuckle—"

The bird-person let out this godawful squak. So very loud that it made my ears buzz.

"No," the bird-person said.

"I got that," I said, shaking my head, and trying to pop my ears to get the buzzing to go away.

"Why doesn't the smell fit?"

I frowned. "I'm not sure I—"

"The place is right," the bird-person prompted. "I am right. So what is not right?"

"Me?" I asked, blinking rapidly and wrinkling up my face as I tried to make at least some sense of this. "How can I be wrong?"

"Wrong?" The bird-person smacked the tip of his staff onto the crystal flooring. Made this series of clicks though its beak that sounded like disapproval. "Who said anything is wrong?"

"But you asked what was not right. Isn't that the same thing?"

"Not at all." The bird-person began walking forward, and walking looked painful. Its foot talons moved with a shuffling kind of step that moved its hips back and forth in a way that made me wince.

Without that staff, the poor thing probably couldn't walk at all.

But the bird-person continued to talk as it walked, and I tried to focus on its words instead of what looked like obvious pain.

"Right and wrong may be opposites in many ways, but to say that all that is not wrong is right, and all that is not right is wrong, that is to overlook the many variations that the universe has given us."

The bird-person stopped in front of me. Reached out and jabbed me in the chest with the point of its staff.

"The universe is full of wonders. To break them all down into mere right and wrong is to overlook their potential."

The bird-person looked up into my face. Those lizard eyes seemed to swirl for a moment.

"This was not the first place you should have stopped. That is why the scent and the look are not synchronized for you, as they should be at all training sites. Does that mean I should dismiss you as wrong? Should I overlook your potential?"

"No?"

"No," the bird-person said, shaking its head once, firmly. "You came here first because your potential and intuition outstripped your understanding."

The bird-person let out this series of caws that I would later learn to consider laughter.

I know. The bird-person was laughing earlier, and now it only issued that series of caws that seemed to amount to the same thing.

Sometimes the bird-person laughed, and sometimes cawed. I never could tell when to expect one or the other.

"I am Trakatak. And though I was slated to be your third teacher, it seems I am to be your *first*."

"I don't suppose that means I'll have an easier time with your lessons?" I asked hopefully. "All that potential?"

That series of caws again.

"Quite the opposite, I fear."

10

I spent months, just studying under Trakatak alone. That's not even counting the rest of my training.

At least, it seems that way. When I try to think back on it.

It *had* to have been *months* of his weird, burning questions — some of them were so outré that I felt as though they literally burned my brain — along with his peculiar exercises of what seemed like a combination of yoga and guided meditation.

Trakatak contorted my body and mind in ways that I'm pretty sure neither was supposed to work.

And yet...

And yet, I never slept during my training. Not with Trakatak, nor with the four other instructors who followed him.

Or her.

Truth be told, I never did learn if Trakatak had a gender, and if so, what it was.

English can be difficult, in that way. The words of English aren't gendered the way they are in some other languages, and yet we have only three pronouns in the third-person singular: he/him, she/her, and it.

It, well, it does apply to the unknown — I've probably used "it" myself when referring to Trakatak now and again — but that word tends to have an ... inanimate connotation to it.

As though the pronoun is supposed to be reserved for objects and not used for people.

Musilancia, the serpentine instructor who was last in my training schedule, taught me languages. Dozens of languages. Scores of them. So very many that I don't think I could begin to list them.

And yet, I understand them all, and can speak and write them with perfect fluency.

I suspect that magic was as involved with that as it was with the rest of my training.

And languages were critical for me, so that I could begin to understand the psychologies and politics of the beings I'd interact with.

Still, Musilancia once used a pronoun to refer to Trakatak that I always thought suited best.

Hris.

Hris is a word in Hrissasstii, the serpentine language most commonly used by nagas, and by about three or four other types of serpent people that frequent the Pacific Northwest.

Hris means, in English, "that person, whose gender is unknown to me, indeterminate, or in transition."

Hris sees a lot of use among serpent peoples who change their gender whenever they want to.

Anyway, I think from now on, when I need a pronoun for Trakatak, and certain others, I'll just use *hris*.

The point is, I never slept during my training. I never ate either. And yet, though I sometimes grew tired, I never felt sleepy. And I never even for a moment felt hungry or thirsty.

I never even had to go to the bathroom.

For the life of me, I wasn't sure time was even passing.

The whole of my training was like a vivid dream. As though I'd had years' worth of experiences within the span of only a few hours. If that.

Snatches of my training come back to me from time to time, but for the most part, I don't really remember the details.

For example, right this second I can remember the exact moment that Oongata, the lime green orangutan-like instructor who followed Trakatak, taught me to temporarily activate an inactive portal.

I'd been standing in front of an iron door, set into Kelly green, slightly glowing crystal. The door had no handle or visible lock. Not even hinges. It just looked like a rectangular sheet of iron, set into the crystal.

It even smelled of iron, just on the edge of beginning to rust. Stark contrast with the pine scent of the crystal rock garden around me.

Oongata had just gone over the procedure for maybe the sixtieth time. Eternal patience in his emerald eyes. His smooth fingers gentle as they corrected my gesture in a way that finally made everything click for me.

I said the word again. *Alethia.* But this time I hit the intonation just right and swirled my fingers with perfect timing.

A shiver lit up my body, like a momentary pulse of static electricity. Every hair on my body stood up.

A flare of white light emanated from my fingertips...

The iron door vanished. Became a swirling series of green lights, contained within the shape of the door.

I hurried through. Felt an echo of that static electricity as I entered.

The portal led only to the iron door's twin on other side of the crystal boulder. Somehow, Oongata was already there, giving me one of his rare smiles and saying...

It's no good.

Oongata told me something then, but I can't remember it now.

The training was all like that. Vivid and real as I experienced it, but then fading like wisps of dream when the alarm clock clatters and the daytime world reasserts itself.

And yet, my instructors had kept me so continually busy with one lesson after the other, that I never even noticed how the previous lesson seemed to fade from my mind the moment it finished.

As though the entirety of my training took place during some untouchable *now*. Some single eternal, yet changeable moment. All without my even noticing.

I didn't understand any of that until Oongata had me open a portal I'd never seen before, even though it sat like a trapdoor right in the middle of his Kelly green rock garden.

I dropped down through the portal...

...and found myself once more in the vast crystal chamber.

The scent of violets. The gently glowing white floor. The ridiculously large round table, with all its roller chairs and other seating arrangements.

The crystal lounge and meeting areas scattered around the wide bottom level of the chamber.

The prismatic pattern of the walls, with the colors of each level arranged in the opposite direction of the floor below it, all the way up to the vast curving walls of the crystal dome, ending in that black circle exactly above the table.

And, of course, the iron doors set into the center of each color. Doors that I knew now had no handles, and needed no handles.

Vasco stood in front of me. Smiling a knowing smile. His long gray hair wild, fitting his animalistic musk. His jeans faded and worn, but holding together. His dull white tee shirt under the red-and-black plaid flannel overshirt.

Duffel bag slung over one shoulder.

Magellan, hopping and barking next to him.

Excited to see me?

"How long was I gone?" I asked, frowning.

"You tell me," Vasco said.

Magellan stopped hopping and barking. Sat and tilted his head as he faced me, as though this were a more important question than it sounded.

My first thought was to say I had no way of knowing. Wasn't as though there were any clocks down here. Calendars either, for that matter.

But I knew I had to at least try to figure out the answer.

I tried to run my mind back over the course of my training, to get some sense of time, but my thoughts couldn't grasp any. As though the mere concept of time simply slipped through my mental fingers.

I opened my mouth to say exactly that, but Vasco lifted an eyebrow.

That was all he did. Raised one eyebrow. And his eyebrows were as wild and gray as the hair on his head (if shorter). Still, I felt as though he was telling me not to fall back on the old kind of answers.

That I actually *did know* the answer. If I *let* myself know it.

And just like that, lessons sprang back through me.

No. Not lessons. Not exactly. The *effects* of the lessons. The teachings I'd incorporated deep inside myself without even knowing I was doing it.

In that instant I realized I could *feel* the flow of time through the great crystal chamber. And it felt ... fluid. As though in ways, time itself ebbed and flowed here. Passing through one color, swirling around through the center of the chamber, then passing back through a different color.

But that was just the surface level. And I needed a more basic sense of time and myself.

The answer lay in my body's age.

I knew how old I was. I mean, I'd seen my birth certificate. I knew that, at least, legally, my parents hadn't just been making up stories when they told me I'd been born in the early days of January, twenty-four years ago.

By reaching inside myself now, I could feel the way time had passed through my body. Like counting the rings of some vast tree.

Twenty-four years, four months, eighteen days, thirteen hours, seven minutes, twenty-six seconds, counting only since my initial exposure to air.

"It's the same day," I said, wonder all through my voice. "But that's—"

"What did Oongata teach you about time through the portals?"

I started to complain that I didn't remember. Except that, just like that, I did.

"Time flows through the many worlds, but not always at the same rates."

I frowned, as more of the lime green orangutan's words came back to me...

Shock hit me like the cold waters of the Willamette. Was that really only a few hours ago?

"And some places," I continued, "time pools so deep that it seems not to pass at all. Even a decade in such a place—"

"Is like no more than a second here." Vasco clapped me on the shoulder. "So. How long have you been gone?"

"Ages," I said, shaking my head as the implications worked their way through me. "But not at all."

Magellan barked approv...

Wait.

Magellan didn't just bark approval. I realized now that where before I could pick up a vague sense of what he meant in his barks, now I could really *understand* him.

Huh. I really did speak Doggerel.

"Perfect!" Magellan barked. "That was the perfect answer. You should get a treat."

"Very good," Vasco said, and clapped me on the shoulder again. "That'll take some getting used to, but we've all been through it. I'd've warned you, but the warning wouldn't have made sense."

"He deserves a treat," Magellan said.

"Hush, you," Vasco said, and tossed Magellan a treat instead.

"Wait," I said, one hand raised as a stop sign. "You dropped a portal on me."

"Yes?" Vasco asked, mischief in his eyes.

"I can't remember everything from my training, but I'm pretty sure no one taught me how to do that."

"What," Vasco said, chuckling. "You thought you'd learn everything your first day?"

My apartment. How long since I last saw it?

I stood there now, just inside my locked front door, on the one-yard square of white tile that amounted to my "entryway."

Hadn't used my keys to get in.

Damn it. The thought of keys now made me chuckle too.

Vasco gave me the evening to myself, to reacclimate to the new me. He and Magellan had then watched as I opened up a temporary portal in one of the iron doors (the one in the center of the red color, though for *this* portal it didn't matter which one I used).

I stepped through, and now I was here. Smelling dinner from my neighbors' place behind me, just across the landing from my front door.

Curry again. I swear, Mandy and Kayla bought curry in bulk. It was a welcome scent, though, because I needed familiarity right now.

I should have been surrounded by the familiar. This was my apartment, after all.

Seven hundred fifty square feet of one-bedroom luxury, all to myself. Laundry cubby, living room, dining room and kitchen all to my right.

Hall closet and bedroom to my left.

Nice, big bathroom straight in front of me.

After the cramped places I'd lived in back in the Bay Area, this apartment had felt downright palatial, the day I moved in.

After all the huge places I'd been today — for however long I'd been those places — my apartment didn't feel too big or too small. It felt ... exactly right for what it was.

And yet, the whole place looked strange to me.

I could see myself everywhere I looked. And yet it had been so long, I almost felt as though I were returning to my college dorm room or something.

To a relic of a past me.

Right here, inside the doorway. Three pegs on the white — "eggshell" as the apartment manager had called it — wall. Pegs occupied by the state of my life as of this morning.

Exhibit one: the heavy, woolen winter coat that Mom had insisted on buying me when she found out where I was moving.

Exhibit two: the hooded windbreaker I'd bought myself, once I got here.

Exhibit three: the "sexy" brown jacket that Katy had gotten me for my birthday.

A few months ago.

A lifetime ago.

Opposite the jackets, my old, beat-up Dr. Strange poster. A Kevin Nowlan drawing, from the 80s.

Heh. Dr. Strange opened portals too. One step closer to my childhood idol.

Time flowed here. This apartment. This world.

I could feel that flow. Smooth and strong. Like the currents of the Willamette, now that I thought about it.

A comparison that reminded me I needed a shower.

It was just me. I stripped off right there in the entryway and walked straight ahead into my bathroom, flicking on the lights as I did. White tile with black trim. Walls and ceiling the same "eggshell" as the rest of the apartment.

Linen cabinet on my left. Followed by the nice, long counter surrounding the sink. Huge rectangle of a mirror. No medicine cabinet, but...

I saw my naked self in the mirror and froze mid-step.

I turned and looked myself over. From the tips of my dark blonde hair to the callused soles of my feet.

For the life of me, I didn't think I looked any different.

I was in good shape, but I knew that. Lots of basketball, plus I swam daily in the kidney-shaped apartment complex pool.

Still, my training had included combat and flexibility. I would have thought I'd...

I stopped. Shook my head. Kicked my fuzzy red throw rug to the side and stood on the cool white tiles, facing my shower-tub.

I bent all the way over backwards, put my hands flat on the tile, and kicked over to a standing position.

I put up my hands and said, "Ta-daaaaaa!"

Well. That was something I definitely couldn't do before. The kick-over I mean. So my body did remember the training. Even if I didn't think I looked any different.

Then again, Vasco was downright skinny. He didn't have the kind of muscles I'd think of for a gymnast. And yet, he was a Locksmith too.

No. I didn't need more questions. I needed a shower, and I needed food.

At the thought of food, my stomach rumbled in a desultory way. As though food sounded like a decent plan, but wasn't critically important.

As I took my shower, I tried to resolve the question of how my mind and body could have undergone all that training — to the point that I had new skills, muscle memories and flexibility — without making me ravenously hungry in the process.

Not to mention dead-on-my-feet tired.

I mean, all that mental and physical work had to have cost me energy, even if time ... wasn't...

Wait. If time wasn't passing, was energy actually expended?

But if time wasn't passing, how could I have changed at all? Didn't change require time, by definition?

By the time I toweled off, I realized I knew the answer. My training had actually covered this.

Change did require time and energy.

However.

Change did not require both in equal measures. Spend enough time, you don't need as much energy. And vice-versa.

Time was the key. And damn it, even that "key" reference made me chuckle.

I stopped and focused on taking deep breaths until the urge to chuckle passed. I was not going to laugh every time I heard or thought the word "keys."

I tried to pretend my deep breaths didn't hitch then, but they did. Despite me.

One of those instructors must have made that joke part of the training. When I remembered who...

The point was, in a place where time pooled deeply, as it did in those places where I trained, energy often abounded.

My training worked through immense amounts of energy. But the time aspect of my training had been banked, by means I wasn't sure I understood.

I knew this much.

That energy — magic, for want of a better word — had also refreshed my body and mind throughout the training, so that I could continue to train without the normal needs for rest and food.

Tricks that worked in those places, but would not work here on earth.

Because here on earth, time flowed at a steady rate. Most locales, anyway.

Now, because the time aspect of my training had been banked, effectively, all the weeks or months or years I *spent* training had taken place in a single instant, the moment I passed through that final portal and returned to the prismatic crystal chamber.

The energy was already committed. Overcommitted, really,

because rather than spending a relatively balanced amount of time and energy — the way change is usually effected here on earth — the process expended immense amounts of energy, such that the total of the change required but a single fraction of a second.

Which would be why my memory of it all was so ... nebulous. Memory, after all, was usually a function of time.

Having concluded that much, I set the issue aside as I slipped into my favorite old red-and-white striped flannel bathrobe. The one I'd gotten for my thirteenth birthday and insisted on keeping.

My robe unquestionably smelled like me.

I picked up my clothes from the entryway tiles, fished my keys out of my shorts pocket and my money out of my shoes, and tossed my clothes — sans shoes — into the laundry bag beside my washer/dryer combo unit.

Barefoot, I padded into the main part of my apartment.

Bookshelves overflowing with science fiction, fantasy and horror. Books as well as movies.

Framed posters for *Star Wars*, *Re-Animator*, and *Army of Darkness*.

Plus, my lone painting. Three feet by four. A castle on a lonely hill. Rendered entirely in textured white paint over black paint, with a single spot of red in a window.

Didn't know the artist. Just spotted it in a shop once and had to have it.

My laptop sat on a huge, solid old teacher's desk I'd picked up for ten bucks at a school auction. On the other side of that desk, the overstuffed dark blue couch I'd been toting around since college, along with the 70s relic of a dark coffee table I'd picked up at the same time.

Then that huge, flat-screen TV. Looked like it was balanced on the head of a pin, but that "pin" was the hexagonal end-table I used as a TV stand.

Too big for the apartment, that television. Looked ridiculous. Blocked part of the glass door that led out onto my little balcony.

Dad's idea. The television. Mom insisted on getting me a coat, so Dad out-did her by getting me a big TV.

If I'd let Mom know, she'd have turned it into an arm's race over who could best help me "start over."

The arm's race thing hadn't been fun, though, since I was sixteen, and I figured out that it had nothing to do with me and everything to do with how they felt about each other.

My smartphone sat on its wireless charger, at the edge of the kitchen's "breakfast bar," which was an opening that led into what would be my dining room.

If I had dining room furniture.

Instead, it was a reading nook. The walls were lined with more bookshelves, surrounding the recliner Rona and Kenzie got me as a going away present.

Nothing competitive about that bit of furniture. They'd gone in together on it at an auction, and I don't think there was much competition for it.

The Beast, as I called it, was burnt orange, padded to hell and back, and big enough to sit two of me. It had a drink holder built into one arm, and could recline perfectly flat.

It looked positively garish, especially under the hanging lamp that belonged above a dining room table.

The Beast's springs complained every time it reclined even the slightest. And it still smelled just a little of cigar smoke.

I loved it.

I snatched my phone off the charger and dropped heavily into the recliner.

Felt like a welcoming hug. Each and every muscle in my back promptly informed me that it had been thoroughly abused and needed rest.

Huh. I didn't feel tired, but my muscles needed rest. Interesting.

So I smiled at the cacophony of tortured springs and reclined to about a forty-five degree angle. The footrest swept my legs up.

I checked my phone.

Nothing.

No calls. No texts. No personal emails. A couple of hits on social media. Probably cat pics or something. Nothing that required my immediate attention though.

So I indulged in ordering a pizza as I planned my evening.

I would eat a pizza covered in pepperoni, black olives, roasted garlic and extra cheese as I watched *The Devil Rides Out* and *Simon, King of the Witches*. Maybe throw in *Bubba Ho-Tep* if I had time.

Three B-movies I knew and loved.

Yes, I knew I was supposed to be spending this evening acclimating. B-movies and pizza were how I acclimated.

I'd have read instead, but I had a sneaking suspicion that I'd be pausing every so many minutes as something or other occurred to me, and I had to get up and try out a move, or test a theory.

That would feel less intrusive to me, watching old movies, than it would if I were reading something off my way-too-big TBR pile.

Plus, it was easier for me to quit movies than books. And I knew I had to make an early night of it.

Vasco had warned me quite clearly that we'd start bright and early the next morning.

Not more training though.

No, tomorrow morning, I was to begin my investigation into why that *riskatan* had been in the Willamette River in downtown Portland.

Fortunately, Vasco and Magellan would come along to support me. Punishment or not, Janna wasn't willing to send a brand new Locksmith out to investigate a problem on his own.

Of course, that made me wonder just how many Locksmiths there were. I remember thinking that Vasco was surprised the prismatic crystal cavern had been so empty when we arrived.

But what did that mean? How many Locksmiths were there?

Enough to fill an eight-top at some local restaurant? Enough to fill a private back room party at that same restaurant?

Enough to fill Pioneer Park at a Timbers or Thorns game?

No way to know. And no way to get answers now.

No, right now it was time for B-movies and pizza.

I needed to decompress and get some sleep.

12

I WAS HAVING THE WEIRDEST DREAM.

I was sitting on a big couch in a coffee shop I'd never been to. I think my mind had pulled it out of an old sitcom.

Sitting next to me was that cute pop singer, Honey Childes. She wore this little black leather number. Something I think she'd worn in a video.

She was explaining the finer points of acoustics and portals, and the importance of precise pronunciation.

Might have been fine. Might have been enjoyable. Except that instead of her usual long, blonde ponytail, she had lime green fur, everywhere I could see.

No one came or went through the glass doors of the coffee shop, either. This steady stream of customers just popped in and out through temporary portals.

And they were all people I knew, from kindergarten, though college and beyond. I think I even saw Jolly and Red show up together, ordering giant glasses of iced tea.

This nebbishy guy behind the counter finally called my order, which didn't make sense because I already had a cup of coffee. Huge, steaming thing. Took two hands to hold.

Made even less sense, really, because I didn't drink coffee.

And yet, I could hear that guy loud and clear.

"Wakey wakey juice for Scott Eagleson! Scott Eagleson. Wakey wakey juice for Scott Eagleson!"

I set down the cup I was already holding.

I got up, but my body was moving too slowly. And the ground was shaking, like a sub-4.0 earthquake — enough to notice, but not enough to care about. Not for a California native like me.

And the guy kept hollering at me, while the quake started ratcheting up the Richter scale. Every step was shaky now. I could even hear the ground trembling, under the sound of the counterman's voice.

"Wakey wakey juice for Scott! Wakey wakey for Scott! Wakey wakey, Scott! Wakey wakey, Scott!"

But it wasn't the nebbishy guy from the sitcom holding out a cup of coffee to me. It was a Kodiak bear. Smelled like it just ran all the way here from Nova Scotia or something.

And the top of the coffee swirled mocha brown energy like a portal...

My eyelids snapped open.

A mass of gray tentacles! Smelling like that dream-bear! Practically right above me!

I found myself reaching for power without knowing how I was doing it...

And then the world began to resolve itself.

Those weren't tentacles.

Even in the pre-dawn gloom of my room with the curtains drawn, I could tell that was hair. Gray hair.

Wild, gray hair.

Which meant the odor wasn't coming from any Kodiak bear.

Which made the skinny person underneath that hair—

"Vasco?" I rumbled through a dry mouth. "Why are you in my room?"

Vasco twisted on my nightstand lamp.

Cold glare and harsh reality.

Vasco was indeed standing beside my bed. But his jeans were black and almost new, and his flannel shirt was a solid forest green. Buttoned up this time, with just a hint of white collar poking out from beneath it. His duffel bag sat on the floor beside him.

"What time is it?" Vasco asked.

"Time to get up!" Magellan barked happily, from somewhere nearby.

"I was asking Scott," Vasco said as I sat up.

Then realized I was naked. I usually do sleep naked, but I don't usually expect to wake up to the sight of an old man and his dog.

I pulled the covers up.

"How should I—" The question died on my lips. Of course I knew the answer. I could feel time flowing all about me. "Five twenty-two—"

I shook my head. "Vasco? Why are you in my room at five twenty-two in the morning?"

"Told you we'd get an early start. Smell like you showered last night, so throw on some clothes. I'll make the coffee."

"I don't have coffee," I called as he and Magellan left the room. "Make tea."

"Cretin," he called back.

I closed the door so I could at least pretend to have some privacy while I dressed.

How should I dress for my first day as an investigatory Locksmith?

I decided to take a cue from Vasco, on that front.

Good, strong blue jeans. White athletic socks. No flannel shirt for me, though. Instead, I went with a short-sleeved silk button up, done in twilight blue.

Stuck with my sneakers. Good all-around shoes, sneakers. I could wear them in any restaurant or museum in Portland without anyone batting an eye, but if I had to fight or run, I knew I could count on them.

By the time I reached the kitchen, the coffee was ready. Smelled rich and dark and entirely unappetizing.

"How can you drink that stuff?" I asked, ignoring entirely that there was now a small, six-cup coffee maker on my counter.

"Coffee is one of this world's great delights," Vasco said. "A gustatory contribution unrivaled by any drinks offered in the west."

I grabbed a black cup with a red chaos symbol out of a cabinet, filled it with water, and shoved it in the microwave to heat while I grabbed a tea ball pre-filled with blackberry tea.

Vasco frowned at me.

"You have a teapot right there." He pointed at it, in its place on the stove.

"And if I wanted more than one cup, I'd use it," I said, rummaging around in the fridge for the breakfast of champions: cold, leftover pizza.

"No," Vasco said, closing the box as I opened it.

I growled at him.

Magellan whined disapproval.

"Look," Vasco said. "One thing you need to remember from your lessons. Everything is related."

I did remember that. But I narrowed my eyes at Vasco all the same.

"Bad enough that you're microwave-heating tea water. The slow rise to boiling of a stove teapot has a different and superior effect on both the water and the taste of the tea."

I started to open the pizza box again. Vasco closed it firmly and kept his hand on the box this time.

"Pizza is fine once in a while," he said. "Back to back meals, though, will influence you in ways you don't expect. Save your cold pizza for dinner tonight. Have something different now. Preferably featuring vegetables and fruits."

He lifted both his hand and an eyebrow.

"Fine," I said, shaking my head as I tossed my leftover pizza back in the fridge. "I don't have—"

I stopped talking, because I'd turned back to see two Denver omelets sitting on the breakfast bar. Both had cucumber slices on the plate, and little bowls of fruit.

The plates and the bowls were brown stoneware that definitely did not come out of my cabinets, which were full of thrifty store dishes and cutlery.

The smell only reached me now. After I'd seen them. Which meant...

What did that mean?

Vasco smiled at me.

The microwave dinged.

"Something you'd like to ask?" Vasco teased as he started into his omelet.

"Fine," I said, throwing the tea ball into my cup hard enough to splash water on the counter. "Where did the coffee maker come from? And the coffee? And these Denver omelets? And these dishes?"

Vasco leaned down and patted his duffel bag. Shoved a forkful of omelet into his mouth.

I started to deny that. Felt the word "no" forming in my mouth, ready to go on to say that there was no way he pulled hot food out of a duffel bag.

Except that he didn't.

The lesson was coming back to me right in that instant. Alustiria. The tall, slender elf woman with the long, platinum hair, tinged with hints of blue...

"The pocket," I said. A shiver of realization flowed over me.

"Exactly," Vasco said. "Each of us has a personal dimension, tied to who we are. Its coordinates are as innate and basic as our fingerprints or our DNA. No two could share the same. And I assume Alustiria taught you to find and access your own?"

"Yeah. We only did that a couple of times, for illustration though."

"No doubt." Vasco sipped his coffee. Pointed at my omelet. "Don't let it get cold."

I started to dig in, and I had to admit that it tasted wonderful. A little heavy on the salt for my taste, but still, quite good.

And the little dish of fruit — slices of apple and orange and persimmon, along with a mixture of berries — tasted even better. As though all of it were fresh-picked.

As I ate, Vasco continued.

"The pocket isn't just an emergency hideaway. It's a great place to store anything you might need, from a few extra bucks to a coffee maker, for example."

"But food," I said, swallowing a mouthful of omelet and sipping some blackberry tea before continuing. "How can you keep food in there without it going bad? Or at least cold? Alustiria said that time in the pocket is tied to our natural rhythms, so it will always flow at the same rate as the world we're from."

"Well," Vasco said, drawing the word out. "I may have applied a couple of other tricks to keep it breakfast-ready. I cooked them about an hour ago."

Magellan chipped in his thoughts.

"I got to eat the extra ham!"

"And some cheddar," Vasco said, shaking his head. "I spoil that dog."

"You're the best!" Magellan barked out. "The best!"

"But why the duffel bag?" I asked.

Vasco chuckled. "Suppose you need to pull something out of your pocket, but you're in a public place."

"Oh," I said. "It's a prop."

"Pretty much. Take a closer look."

Yesterday I wouldn't have known what that meant, beyond the literal.

Today I knew that by asking me to take a closer look, Vasco was telling me to look beyond my normal senses.

And now that I could do that, I could tell that within the duffel bag played a series of energies that I now thought of as magic. I couldn't quite gauge what these did, but realization slapped me in the face.

"My shirt," I said. "That wasn't a replacement. You ... how did you manage to grab my shirt and repair it without my noticing?"

"You were more than a little distracted yesterday. I could have walked a five hundred pound gorilla right in front of you without your noticing, if I'd timed it right."

I looked down at Magellan.

"He didn't, did he?"

"That would be telling," Magellan barked.

Vasco laughed.

I pushed forward my empty plate. Must have been hungrier than I thought. I knocked back the last of my blackberry tea, set down my cup with authority.

"Ready to go then?" Vasco asked.

A frenzy of nerves whirled through my guts. But I had a smile on my face.

"Let's do this."

13

I'D ASSUMED OUR FIRST STOP WOULD HAVE BEEN NEAR THE *RISKATAN* attack. That maybe something about that location was the answer.

But Vasco made it clear before we left: Locksmiths had already checked for the easy, obvious answers.

Nothing wrong had happened simultaneous to the attack. Not in the greater Portland area, at least.

And there appeared to be nothing special about the *dorach* or the place the *dorach* was attacked.

Thus, our first stop was someplace I didn't know. Someplace cold and wet.

But then, any riverbank is a chilly place to be standing when dawn breaks. Especially in Portland in the springtime.

At least, I was pretty sure we were still in Portland. I could make out an industrial area across the broad river, but that could have been Vancouver for all I knew.

Green trees — maples, or at least that's what a glance suggested to me — and grass up the bank behind me, but I was as likely to find those in Washington as Oregon.

I did know that the wet sand under my sneakers was brown, and the cold river spray on my face did at least as much to wake me up as the blackberry tea had done.

And I was starting to think that my silk shirt was a poor choice.

Certainly Vasco, who knelt on the sand beside me, didn't seem to be as bothered by the cold or wet in his flannel shirt.

Magellan seemed downright pleased to be here, running back and forth behind us — kicking up sand, of course — and yapping about nothing in particular. Except maybe joy to be outside in the morning.

"Vasco?" I asked.

"Hmmm?"

"Where are we?"

"Oh, right." Vasco stood and brushed sand from his hands. He pointed off to my left, down the shore a ways.

"Follow that direction," he said, "and you'll get to Fred's Marina. Nice little place to stop for fuel and food, if you like boating."

He pointed at the river ahead of us.

"I assume I don't have to tell you which river that is?"

I looked at it. It forked a few hundred feet further northwest from where we stood. But I couldn't tell by sight nor smell if this was the Willamette, the Columbia, or something else.

I gave him a sheepish grin.

Vasco sighed.

He pointed right. "The Willamette comes in along here." Pointed further up the flow. "It continues off to the north there, but splits into the Multnomah Channel off to the northwest."

He cocked an eyebrow at me. "Do you at least know the name of the island formed by that channel?"

"I just moved here," I said.

Vasco sighed and shook his head. "Magellan?"

"Sauvie Island," Magellan barked.

Vasco tossed him a treat. Looked back at me. "That's Portland ahead of us across the river, and behind us on the other side of those trees. You understand that much?"

"Of course," I said. "So we're here because this is the first place the Willamette splits?"

"First place this close to Portland," Vasco corrected. "Which means it's the last line of defense against any river creatures that are allowed in the Columbia, but not this part of the Willamette."

"Are there..." I started, but realized I knew the answer. There were sixteen types of creature allowed in the Columbia but not the Willamette. At least, this near to Portland.

I swear, Vasco's eyes twinkled as he saw me recall the answer to the question I almost asked.

"So why are we here?" Vasco asked me.

"Because there should be some kind of barrier or ward here? Enforcing the treaties?"

"And is there?"

I blew out a breath and shook my shoulders. My first real test.

I looked out across the river.

No. That's not quite right.

I stretched my awareness out across the river.

That involved looking, but honestly, it was more than that. It was as though I reached out with a portion of my mind and sifted along the edges of reality through the section of river ahead of me.

I had a vague sense of what I was looking for, so I didn't get distracted by the other things I detected. A trio of spirits floating along above the river itself, two dead sailors and one ... river spirit, I was pretty sure. It had a ... watery feel to it, and its shape flowed and shifted in ways the dead sailors didn't.

I'd have to look closer to know what variety of water spirit, but that wasn't my focus right now.

Instead I let my mind sink under the water.

Normal river life...

A lizardfolk, of the type known to us as Sissalaxa. Smooth, teal skin and a long, thick tail. Eyes like a gecko, but webbed fingers and toes. I could call him over to us if I wanted. Ask him questions. But he looked as though he were out for an early morning swim, and maybe a breakfast fish or two.

There.

I spotted what I was looking for, and the moment I did it snapped into clear focus.

It was as though someone had stretched a chain net through the Willamette River. Except that the links of the chain were made from a shimmering, reddish-orange type of energy.

And the chain net didn't seem to interact with anything. Fish and snakes swam right through it. So did the lizardfolk.

Still, I was pretty sure I was looking at a barrier that should have held back the *riskatan*.

"Yes," I said. "It's there. And from here, it looks intact."

"Do you need to get closer to be sure?" Vasco asked.

I thought about that, and shook my head when I realized that I could detect more than the sight of the chain net.

I could hear and feel a vibration from it. A subtle tonic chord that seemed harmonious in a way that implied to me that the net was intact.

"No," I said, with a firm shake of my head. "No, it sounds right to me, and it looks right. The only thing I could check is its feel, and since there's nothing off in its look and its tone, the feel should be fine."

Vasco shook his head.

"Not good enough," he said. "That's only two out of three. And is that all there should be?"

"What, you want me to lick the chain net?"

"No," Vasco said, chuckling. "Amusing an image as that would present. Magellan, how does it smell?"

"Smells like fresh, healthy pig's blood," Magellan said.

Vasco laughed at the look on my face.

"That's right," he said. "And no, it's not because pig's blood was used in forging the chain. It's a sign of how Magellan detects and interacts with the energies we work with."

He crouched and scratched the beagle's head.

"How would it smell if there was a problem?"

"Sick," Magellan barked, tail going a mile a minute and his head high and proud. "Diseased."

"So smell confirms what you see and hear," Vasco said. "Is that enough?"

"Well, the vibrations I can feel ... I need to touch it, don't I?"

"Do you?"

"Yes," I said with a sigh. "You should have told me I'd be getting my shirt wet."

Vasco laughed as we strolled down the beach to the nearest point of the chain net. He shook his head at me.

I saw what he was doing then. The chain net extended into the ground. Into the sand.

I trotted over to the spot before he reached it. Stuck my hand down into the wet, heavy sand. Burrowed my way down a few inches to what I needed.

I could feel the chain net now. Buzzing with vibrant energies. But there was a ... a sense of limit to it. Completeness. Wholeness.

I stood up and clapped my hand clean. Smoothed the sand with my sneaker.

"Feels right," I said. "If this is the last line of defense, it's intact, and not how the *riskatan* got through."

"Fair enough," he said. "And your shirt is still dry."

I chose not to point out that river spray had dampened it a darker color.

"Wait," I said as Vasco turned away.

Vasco turned back to me, one wild gray eyebrow high.

"The *riskatan* didn't break through this chain net. But if the chain net didn't recognize the *riskatan*, it could have passed through as easily as that Sissalaxa did a few minutes ago."

Vasco gave me a slow smile. "Now you're thinking like a Locksmith."

My shoulders slumped. "You'd already thought of that, hadn't you?"

"Yes," he admitted. "But it was still good that you thought of it now. If you hadn't thought of it after we checked the next two barriers, I'd've said something then."

"Two barriers," I said. "One where the Willamette meets the Columbia, and one where the Multnomah Channel meets the Columbia?"

"Exactly."

"He should get a treat," Magellan barked.

Vasco didn't give me a treat, though I didn't feel as put out about that as Magellan did.

Vasco used temporary portals to get us to the other two barriers, but the results were the same in both places.

Right now we were standing among the sharp rocks and gray sandy dirt of Kelley Point, staring out across the Columbia River at Washington.

Stronger wind here. Chillier. Cutting back and forth in a way I'd only experienced before on the beaches of Santa Cruz and Half Moon Bay, back in the greater Bay Area.

Well, down on Pier 39 in SF, too, but only right by the water.

Here it wasn't salt water in the spray though, which made it more pleasant. Though any hope I'd had of keeping my silk shirt even passably dry was gone.

My hair was a mess too, but that wasn't likely to be important.

By now the sun was fully visible out east, and the morning sky looked a lot more blue than gray. Apart from a scattering of morning clouds, at least.

I could hear car traffic in the distance, and hear and see the beginnings of boat traffic closer.

The barrier here was off to our left, sealing off the Willamette from those who, by treaty, were not allowed down it.

"Well," Vasco said with a sigh. "It was too much to hope that the answer would be so simple as that."

"You should be glad," I said. "If those barriers were down, there'd be more trouble than a single *riskatan*."

Vasco cocked an eyebrow at me.

"Right," I said. "That the *riskatan* didn't get here on its own—"

"—proves that there's more trouble," Vasco finished. "Still, they had to be checked."

"No they didn't," I said.

Vasco turned to me, wild eyebrows high. Magellan's tail was going a mile-a-minute, but he was sitting still and staring at me, excitement all through his eyes.

"You, or someone else, checked them already." I shrugged. "You wouldn't have waited for me. Not if other things could have been slipping through and causing trouble."

"He's good," Magellan barked.

Vasco smiled and clapped me on the shoulder. "So why did I take you to check the barriers anyway?"

"To settle my nerves and let me try a few basic things without anyone watching?"

"Yes," Vasco admitted without a trace of shame. "But also because you needed to experience the barriers for yourself. Knowledge is one thing. Experience is another."

I nodded, not entirely sure I agreed — knowledge, to me, implied experience, otherwise it was just information — but I didn't want to debate the issue right here.

Especially not with the early joggers on the trail not a few hundred feet behind us.

"So," Vasco said, giving me an evil grin. "The obvious answer isn't the solution, Locksmith. And we're now into unchecked territory. What comes next?"

"The nearest portal to the place that I spotted the *riskatan* has to be checked."

"And that is?"

"Ross Island."

"Then I trust you can get us there."

14

THE ROSS ISLAND PORTAL WASN'T ACTUALLY ON ROSS ISLAND.

Apparently, nobody wanted to call it the "Toe Island Portal."

That's right. I said "Toe Island."

See, there was this small chain of four islands in the middle of the Willamette River, just south of central Portland.

Well, *three* islands, really, but I'll get to the why of that in a second.

The biggest of these islands, of course, was Ross Island.

Ross Island looked kind of like a great big fishhook — acres and acres of fishhook — when viewed from above. And from above was the only way I'd seen it at that point. Pictures on the internet, and the occasional glance as I passed on the nearby Ross Island Bridge.

The Ross Island Bridge didn't actually go to Ross Island, which says a lot about what it's like trying to get around Portland without a GPS.

But I'm getting off track.

Now *technically* Hardtack Island was the second biggest of this little chain.

However.

At some point it got connected to Ross Island by levee. I think it was to form a lagoon, and make work easier on the miners and dredgers. Something like that.

Whatever the reason, because of that levee I consider it all part of Ross Island and will not acknowledge "Hardtack Island" as separate.

Largely because without Hardtack Island, Ross Island has no hook, and I can't describe it as a fishhook. Which I think is a charming image.

So. *Three* islands in the small chain. Don't let the internet tell you differently.

Anyway, southeast of *Ross* Island is East Island. Looks kind of like a spade in a deck of playing cards, except it's all green. A private island of some kind, which made me immediately suspect it was some villain's evil lair.

I mean, what would be the point of having a private island that looks like a nature preserve with no visible construction, unless it was actually a front for some kind of secret lair?

Anyway, southwest of Ross Island was a rock.

All right, it was a big rock.

Maybe only a tenth the size of East Island, and maybe a hundredth the size of Ross Island. Still, it was considered big enough to merit getting called an island in its own right. Much the way Pluto was considered big enough to get called a planet.

Depending on whom you asked. And when.

This big rock was shaped kind of like a banana, with the stem at the north end. A few odd, scattered shrubs, mainly in the middle, but primarily it was all just rock and dirt.

Didn't look like a toe at all, in my humble opinion. And yet, it got designated Toe Island somewhere along the line, by someone who was allergic to bananas.

All right, that's speculation on my part. But it really should have been called Banana Island.

Or better still, Banana Rock.

Then again, "Banana Rock Portal" would have sounded even sillier.

Nevertheless, that was where I took us from Kelley Point. A quick jaunt through a mud-brown portal, because existing portals are the easiest things to travel to.

Four portal jaunts already this morning, one by my own hand, and the sun was only really just now up in the sky.

Must sound as though I was already a jaded old hand at traveling by portal.

That's not true at all though.

I mean, I understood how to do it. And in the process of training, I'd probably traveled by portal thousands of times.

But that training, all those portals, that experience was hiding somewhere in the back of my subconscious, waiting for the right kind of trigger to bring it to the surface.

Which meant that, on a conscious level, I was still pretty darned new to all of this.

Opening that portal, back at the tip of Kelly Point? It had been exciting. The way my fingers tingled as the energies flowed through me and outward, spiraling into the circular shape of the portal.

The subtle vibration of the undertones of the word "alethia" that changed it from a normal word to a word of power.

The electric charge to the air.

The smell of clover honey.

Honestly, it felt so good, it was like something I shouldn't get caught doing in public. Might have even tried to find someplace where I wouldn't be seen opening it.

Except Vasco reminded me that portals are the kinds of things that most people don't want to notice. So they don't.

And sure enough, the moment I began, the joggers looked away. Even the woman sailing her own little sloop — the woman who'd waved at me only moments before — turned away as I started focusing energy.

If anyone *had* seen me, say, from a distance, or out of the corner of their eye?

Whatever they saw they probably would have dismissed as a trick of the light. And if they didn't dismiss the sight, who knew? Might have had the makings of a future Locksmith.

Anyway, we stepped through that portal and out of the connection to the Ross Island Portal, there at the northern tip of the banana stem, on Toe Island.

More chilly wind and wet spray.

This poor silk shirt was done for, and it wasn't even noon yet. The waters of the Willamette churned high from the nearby passage of a tugboat.

Wasn't pulling anything. Might not have been in service. Not very big either. Just the one smallish cabin above a raised portion of the deck, and a hook hanging out behind it. No more than a half-dozen tires strapped to the side, for whatever reason people strapped tires to a boat.

Tugboat sure wasn't in great shape. Smelled like a tire fire. I could see rust here and there under faded red and blue paint. Even the name — the Grinder — was only just visible over what looked to have been at least a dozen previous names.

Three people up on deck. One bearded man — and in Portland, that meant his beard bushed out dark inches away from his chin and cheeks — in shorts and a white tee shirt with some kind of logo. He also had on a dark, Hillsboro Hops baseball cap. The two others up there were in yellow slickers. Pants and jackets.

With the hoods up.

Something about that nagged at me.

They were up a dozen feet or so above where I stood. Couldn't have gotten hit by that much river spray. Not enough to merit that much rain gear. And there sure was no sign of rain in the mostly clear sky above.

What was more, the day was shaping up to get back into the 80s again, which meant that slickers like those would be too hot before even noon.

I looked closer as they passed.

They were bulky people, the ones in the slickers. The man with the shorts was skinnier. Not much older than I was. Tanned and weathered, though, as though he lived on his boat.

I started to stretch more of my awareness out toward the boat.

Vasco cleared his throat.

I shook my head. Whirled on him.

"Did you see them?" I pointed at the tugboat, but Vasco lowered my hand.

"Portals and spells are one thing," he said. "Pointing is something *everyone* notices."

"But—"

"As for who or what are wearing yellow rain gear on the tugboat that just passed us, how many nonhuman people are there in Portland proper on an average day?"

"Three thousand, give or take." The answer popped out before I could even have given it a thought. "But—"

"But we have more important work to do here, don't we? Or shall we bother every one of those three thousand people? Is that how you wish to spend your time investigating this problem, Locksmith?"

"No," I said, though the word tasted a little bitter. Made me wince as I said it.

I flared my nostrils in a deep sigh and turned to look at the portal.

The Ross Island Portal had come to my mind because it was the closest portal to where I'd seen the *riskatan*. That was true. But it had also come to mind because it was the nearest portal close to the water line of the Willamette River.

Right here at the stub of the toe, as it were. Or, as I preferred it, right at the tip of the banana's stem. The very northern end of the dirty rock that got called an island.

Just above the waterline, maybe a half-dozen feet from the waters of the Willamette, jutted up a big slab of brownish gray rock. Looked random. Broader than it was tall. Gentle slope up the back side, for an easy path to its top edge.

The kind of rock that would be good to sit on while eating a bag lunch, watching the water, and pondering life.

On the steep side of that rock, though, a four-foot diameter section was the location of one of those thin spots in the universe.

A natural portal.

Felt like slate under my fingers, but it probably would have felt that way even if there wasn't an ounce of slate in that whole island.

Something about the presence of a portal gave rock a slatish kind of feel. One of the ways they could be recognized.

Vasco watched as I slid my fingers across the tiny ridges of that slate. He stood perfectly still. So still that out of the corner of my eye, he seemed to have turned into a statue.

If it weren't for the wind tossing his wild gray hair, I might have thought he *was* a statue.

On my other side, Magellan sat. Tail wagging, and head tilted. Fascinated, as I did my thing.

I placed my left hand in the center of the four-foot portal radius. I had to crouch a bit, but that was fine.

My right hand, I pointed down. Not pointing with my fingers, just the whole of my hand. And not pointing at the rock, either.

Through the rock. Through the universe itself. Down into the depths of the Underworld. The primal place. A core source of power and emotion. History. Ties to all that has come before.

I felt the connection through my right hand.

Warmth flooded my fingertips. Workout warmth. Hot tub warmth. The warmth of relaxed readiness.

Up my fingers that sensation spread.

Into my arm. My shoulder.

It seeped through my body. Filled me up. A heady, powerful kind of readiness.

Into my left arm now. Flowing down, down, all the way to my fingers.

When I could feel that sensation itching even at the fingertips of my left hand — that eagerness to act — only then was it time for the gesture and incantation.

I let the middle two fingers of my left hand bend inward to touch my palm. My index finger and pinkie twirled opposing circles.

"Apokalypto," I intoned, and the word vibrated out of me as though it started down in my spine instead of my diaphragm.

The portal sprang to life. Swirling cherry red and midnight blue in opposing directions.

The scent of hyacinth filled the air. Stronger even that the clean smells of the Willamette, or the polluting odors of that tugboat.

And the past seventy-two hours of the portal swirled within those red and blue colors.

Reading that history had been a class of its own. It didn't come through in nice, pretty pictures. No.

It was like reading tea leaves. Or maybe like finding pictures in clouds, or a field of static.

Except that the most important element was personal quiet.

Reading the history accurately meant ensuring that the Locksmith didn't look for what he wanted to see. He had to see what presented itself.

So, while I had all that heady power flowing through me from the Underworld, I had to keep my thoughts and opinions to myself. Keep my breathing steady. And just stare into what was there.

To look into those swirling reds and blues, and allow pictures and symbols to form on their own...

15

MY WORLD, A SWIRL OF CHERRY RED AND MIDNIGHT BLUE. THE CHERRY red flowing clockwise. The midnight blue, anticlockwise.

Sounds in my ears. Buzzing. Like a small swarm of bees on each side of my head, flitting about and trying to convey some message that I didn't have the pheromone receptors to pick up.

The smell was hyacinth. Everywhere. So strong in my nose, it was as though I'd fallen into a field of hyacinths face first. Sweet and subtle?

Not in this case.

In this case, it was sweet and overwhelming. Drove away the taste of that Denver omelet breakfast I'd had, along with any remaining hints of my blackberry tea.

No wet chill in the air though. If I was, in fact, feeling any air. I certainly felt no breeze.

Instead, just a steady warmth. Like an 80 degree day under a cloudless sky, when the wind just seemed to give up.

All of this was information. All of it was relevant.

I just had to figure out how.

The answer would lie in those swirls of red and blue.

Counterpoint, they flowed. Speeds varying. Breadth of each bar varying. Sometimes the red would flow so wide and thick that the blue seemed to vanish.

Other times, the blue seemed to swallow up the red, leaving not so much as a trace.

And all of this was information. I just needed to know if...

No.

No questions. Not now.

No questions. No opinions.

I needed to become a passive reflector of what I perceived. A mirror, onto which the past seventy-two hours could shine out their history, as related to this portal.

I would draw a centering breath, but I had no breath to focus on. I could not feel my lungs, or my nose. I could not even feel the surge of power I'd pulled up from the Underworld. Not now. Not here.

Oh, I could stretch for those feelings, if I chose. But that would have been a choice.

And right now, I needed only to observe.

So I watched. And smelled. I listened. And felt.

I even tasted the air, if that was air, to determine if I could get any character to the hyacinth fragrance, beyond what my nostrils were picking up.

If I was really picking up anything through my nostrils. It might have all been coming in through my mind.

I wasn't clear on that part. Seeking the answer right now would only have been a distraction.

So I perceived and waited. Allowed the patterns to establish themselves.

And, over time, understanding grew within me.

The hyacinth smell. It was the scent of the energies of this particular portal. And that it seemed to carry no undersmell, that meant that no magics had been performed on it that might modify it in any way.

I almost lost focus there. The idea of something modifying a portal without the Locksmiths knowing — and Vasco would have told me if he'd known of this portal being modified recently — that was a scary idea.

But it wasn't what happened.

Back to figuring out what *did* happen.

I needed a moment to clear my mind again. To let the impressions flow over me once more, without my mind stressing over things that had not occured.

The portal had not been modified. That was good, useful information.

The sound of the buzzing. That was the energies of this portal, and how they interacted with this part of our universe.

I *thought* they felt unchanged. Normal, more or less. I couldn't detect any variations that might have indicated something as wrong.

But, this was my first experience with this portal. And experience, as I'd said, was different from information.

Still, I thought that the energies of the portal seemed to be interacting normally with the universe.

So nothing had happened to warp the portal, as it related to the fabric of the universe.

Yes, that sounded a lot like the information I got from the scent, but it wasn't quite the same thing. The portal itself could be modified, without modifying how it interacted with the fabric of reality.

The obverse was true as well. For example, it might have been possible to move a portal.

Oh, it would take immense amounts of power, and draw lots of attention, but it was the most obvious example I could think of for how the portal's relationship with reality could be modified without otherwise affecting the portal's magic.

So, what mattered here was that nothing in the sound or smell told me that anything out of the ordinary had occurred.

That much, as least, was good.

It might have been expected, if I'd allowed myself expectations.

Instead, I focused on the feel of the temperature.

It felt a little warm to me.

That meant something.

I had to slam my thoughts shut quick before speculation came over me.

I did my level best, instead, to focus on the sensation of that temperature.

Warm, but not hot. Warm, but not tepid.

Warm, but still...

No. The stillness was not at issue here. The feel had to be still because the scent and sound indicated no attempts to modify the portal or its relationship with reality.

Had there been an attempt, I would have felt motion, giving me a greater sense of what and how.

So the *temperature* was what mattered.

Warm...

The answer flooded back out of my training memories.

Warm meant the portal had been used within the past seventy-two hours.

Finally! Something...

No. No conclusions. No opinions. Not yet.

The portal had been used. Not heavily used. That would have been hot, not warm.

Still, someone or something had used this portal recently.

And any more information would come down to sight.

Somewhere within those swirling reds and blues was the answer to who or what had used the portal, and what they'd done with it.

I stared into the swirling colors. Allowed the rhythm of their flow wash over me. I might have begun to sway with that rhythm. I can't be sure.

The pulses of color that shifted the breadth of each bar of cherry red and midnight blue, they had meaning.

The pulses. The breadth. They told a story...

That story, it was of the portal opening twice...

The first time. Two and a half days ago.

Yes! Now that I'd given myself over to the flow of the colors, I could feel them show me when and how the portal had been used.

Sixty hours ago. Give or take.

Late afternoon sun. Heavy clouds rushing past far overhead.

A leprechaun stepped through the portal. Only as tall as my knee. The shock of his coppery hair and beard a stark contrast to the black of his suit with its greenish trim.

Stocky, this leprechaun. And old, despite the color of his hair.

Glasses. Pince-nez. Gold rimmed.

He carried something. Cackled his glee.

He carried a stone. Greenish gray. Needed both hands to do it. Rounded and smooth, this stone, but flat. Flat enough it almost had an edge.

He tossed that stone onto the waters of the Willamette, where it floated.

The leprechaun jumped onto it like a surfboard.

The leprechaun faded from my mind. Too distant now. His further actions unrelated to the portal.

I thought the leprechaun looked to be heading east toward Selwood, but I wasn't sure.

Back into the swirl of colors.

They shifted with *time*, I understood now. Ebbing and flowing their pace between this location and the other end of the portal's natural link.

The other end, I knew, was known to Locksmiths as Gehnach. a place of sand and darkness. Heat. Fires in the night sky, and erupting from the sands themselves.

But that didn't matter. Not right now.

My mind flowed forward with the swirl of the portal. Followed its period of inactivity, that harmonized with the buzzing in my ears.

Felt cooler, those periods of inactivity. And the time that the leprechaun had come through, the portal had warmed further, though my attention had been on sight, and I'd missed...

Now.

Again, something using the portal.

Twenty-four hours ago.

Rain in the air, but fading with the dawn. Fading with the slight misting of the night before.

Gentle morning wind. Gentler than today's.

Portal activated from this end.

A person standing in front of the portal.

Tall and slender. Cloaked and hooded. Boots that came to the knee, a dark leather of some kind.

Couldn't tell male or female, so I defaulted again to the Hrissasstii pronoun *hris*.

This person had *hris* left hand forward. Completed a gesture much like the one I would have used to activate the portal.

Long, slender fingers. A little long to be human, which meant I couldn't guess what the slenderness might mean.

Skin looked pretty close to human though. Pale end of Caucasian, it looked to me. Certainly made *me* look tan.

Suddenly the cloaked person stood straight. *Hris* shoulders came up.

Elegant hands reached out wide. Called together hot energy. Energy that felt baked in the sun on hot concrete. Or was that the smell?

Those hands came together...

Something slapped my face hard enough to make my ears ring.

I was standing once more on the rocky stem of Banana Island. I mean Toe Island. Facing the rock that held the portal, which was now closed.

I could smell the Willamette River. Feel tension sing through my body.

The lovely relaxed energy I'd tapped from the Underworld? Gone.

In its place, a discombobulation. Uncertainty. Was I standing here? Or was I still in my kitchen? Eating an omelet. Drinking my tea...

The shock of the slap once more. Not the sensation. My cheek still sang with that. No, but the shock of the blow. Or its echo.

I staggered backward.

Might have fallen in the water, except that Vasco's strong hand grabbed my arm and stopped me.

"Let me see," he said, leaning in and pushing my left hand away from my face.

My face was still hot, stinging.

My ears rang. I could hear my blood rushing as well. Underneath that, if I tried — which I did by a reflex that was new to me — I could hear the rushing wind and the distant noise of traffic. The muttering of Vasco. The worried whine of Magellan.

More concerning to me was the heavy pounding of my heart.

"Bleeding," Magellan barked.

"Obviously," Vasco said, voice distant. He slung down his duffel bag. Rummaged through it while frowning at my face.

"What do you mean I'm bleeding?"

"Bleeding," Magellan barked again. He sounded worried. Pawed back and forth in the dirt behind me.

"Magellan means someone managed to slap you down during your investigation."

"Literally," I said. "Wasn't a move I recognized. Not even now that I've had a moment for memories to come back to me."

"Wait," Vasco said.

He slathered a little smelly green paste on my cheek, then started rubbing it vigorously.

Hot pain made me cry out before I could stop myself.

"Quit whining," Vasco said, voice a little distant with focus.

Whining, he called it. My face felt like he was pressing an inch of hot solder to my cheek.

I clenched my teeth and breathed through my mouth. Helped with the rank herbal odor of the goop.

Didn't help with the hot pain. That was just...

...gone?

I blinked at Vasco, and he chuckled and tucked a small jar back into his duffel bag.

"What was..." I stopped.

Vasco didn't answer. Just let my memories tell me.

That was a healing concoction known as Serpent's Kiss, because its main ingredient was a poisonous venom. Well treated with other herbs, but still.

Nothing better for cuts. Forced the skin to reknit at breakneck speeds. Hurt like hell, but did the job.

I'd had lessons in alchemy?

"So what did you pick up?" Vasco leaned back against the big rock, just to my left of the portal zone.

I told him, starting with the leprechaun and finishing with the gesture.

"Go over the second activation again. Every detail you can remember."

I did. Didn't say anything differently from the first recitation, which made Vasco frown.

"You lost focus," he said. "Made comparisons to your own skin. That was how she noticed you."

"She? You know who this is?"

"I do." Vasco frowned through a slow breath that flared his nostrils. "And it's not good."

16

I'D WONDERED WHAT THE BIG, PRISMATIC CRYSTAL CAVERN LOOKED LIKE when it was busy?

This was my chance to find out.

Whoever or whatever this woman was, she was a big enough, bad enough deal that Vasco wanted us to go report in to Janna *right now*.

He fired up the Ross Island Portal, but shifted its endpoint. Took us to the passage in Mount Hood. Down the long hall again that smelled slightly like roses.

Then through the black marble archway shot through with gold, and into the vast crystal cavern.

One might ask why, if this was such a big deal, we didn't save time and portal directly into the crystal cavern?

I did ask.

Turned out that it was impossible to portal into the crystal cavern, except by a very few, specific routes.

Each Locksmith was taught one route in.

Vasco, as Lockmaster, knew three.

Only Janna knew how many total paths in there were, or how to access them all. That was part of the reason she was the Lady of Portals.

When we stepped out of that doorway and into the crystal cavern — I'm sure it only *felt* as though we'd been walking through that hallway for hours — it was busy as Pioneer Square on a weekend day.

Conversation was riotous and impossible to distinguish. Partially because there were so many languages being spoken at the same time. Partially, just because the magic of the cavern leant itself toward privacy, in a way that made conversations echo beyond clarity.

At least, when multiple conversations were underway.

Right now, the seven levels of the crystal cavern were all in use. And every use looked formal.

From what I could tell, there were Locksmiths — and I was sure of that only because they were in pairs and human — interviewing people in various crystal lounges, spread across the ringed levels.

The prismatic colors of the walls. I noticed almost immediately that they were rotating faster now. Fast as a second hand, each level the opposite direction as the one above it.

And I didn't know why they moved so fast.

That little detail on its own was so unexpected — that I actually had a question that didn't seem to be answered by a sudden flood of memory — I had to stop two steps inside the door from the hallway under Mount Hood. Had to stop, mid-step and say, "The colors. Why—"

"They're always moving," Vasco said, dismissively. "Most of the time it's so slow that you wouldn't notice unless you tried. But right now, it's too active in here."

That wasn't nearly enough of an answer for me, but Vasco changed subjects.

He muttered something to Magellan that I didn't pick up. Pointed to an interview two levels down, where a pair of young women in black suits were asking questions of...

...a big, yellow and black bat creature.

"Is that Chiron?"

"Hmm?" Vasco said, even as Magellan barked a denial.

"No," Vasco said, shaking his head gently and hurrying me along down the stairs — that also moved, along with the colors — "that's his second in command. K'lakak."

"Why—"

"No way to know that," Vasco said. "Not for sure."

He cleared his throat. "No more questions right now. We have more important things to worry about than what other Locksmiths are doing."

And so I held back any further questions, and just marveled at the variety of life forms here in the crystal chamber as I followed Vasco down another level.

More varieties of lizard folk. At least four that I could spot.

One big brown bear that had dark green tentacles coming out of its back.

A trio of huge raccoons. Easily six-feet tall, and at least half that broad. One wore a bandolier of some kind, and all three appeared deep in conversation, while waiting for ... there. A fourth who was being interviewed.

The next level down, a collection of shadows that seemed to be one individual, based on the way they chased each other.

Along similar lines, one white crystal couch appeared to be occupied by a shifting, hairy individual that looked like a tall, thick human, whose pelt was ridiculously varied in colors...

...that also moved.

That was when I realized that what I'd thought was a single entity appeared to be a moving swarm of rats, all comprising a single creature.

No memories around this one.

"What is that?"

I asked. Couldn't help it.

"Oh, the Rodenton? Just what it looks like." Vasco shrugged, and hurried me down another set of stairs, from a fern fragrance to an icy aroma.

"Rodentons," Vasco continued, speaking softly so I had to keep up if I wanted to hear him, "are good fellows, whether acting as individual rats, or collectively. They are capable of forming a hive mind, you see."

"And they're good folks?" Not sure I understood what that meant.

"Quite friendly," Magellan added. "A few will even play fetch with me."

"Helps that you bring them back gently," Vasco said. "They throw parts of their collective, and Magellan chases them down and carries them back."

"They make a whole separate game of reattaching." The tail started going faster. "Think they'll play with me now?"

"No," Vasco said. "Looks to me that they're in the middle of providing some pretty valuable intel. Wonder if it's about the bar matter..."

"Bar matter?"

Vasco frowned at me, and hustled me faster as we moved down another flight of stairs to the scent of lilacs.

"Just some strange goings on behind some eastside bars. Rodentons often have great information about what goes on around bars."

I didn't get to ask any follow-up questions there, because we finally made it down to the last level, and the smell of violets.

This was the only level not teeming with activity.

Janna was right now parked at the gigantic round table, apparently having a heated argument with a trio of pale, white-haired elves in ivory robes.

From their look and garb, I guessed them to be from Lisatasa, an elvish community that's been making use of the Upper Forest Park Portal for the last hundred years or so.

Janna herself had dressed for the occasion in a deep purple sundress.

Still, conversation couldn't have been possible. The elves were on the other side of the table. I mean, the acoustics...

...were probably magically tuned for just this sort of situation.

I realized then that I could see Janna gesturing as she spoke most emphatically, but I couldn't hear so much as a whisper from her.

And these were the only people down on this level.

"Better let her finish," Vasco said, taking me by the shoulder and leading me to a set of crystal couches that were surprisingly comfortable.

Magellan trotted over to Janna, presumably to tell her we were here and waiting.

Once we were settled, I gestured to the various conversations going on, on the levels above us.

"Are all those people Locksmiths?" I asked.

"The humans?" Vasco nodded. "Yes. Now that you've joined us, we have an even two dozen in the greater Portland area. And most of them are here right now."

He snorted. Shook his head. "Too many things going on all at once. She's got to be behind it."

"The person I saw at the Ross Island Portal?"

Vasco nodded.

"Who is she?"

"Wait," he said.

I had to gnash my teeth at that one, but I waited. Drumming my fingers on a soft, softly glowing, white crystal armrest.

Magellan trotted back, and barked that he'd told Janna we were here.

The thoughtful beagle noted my impatience, and produced a blue rubber bone from ... somewhere. He jumped up on the couch next to me. He sat up, paws high and proud, and tail going at record-breaking speeds.

"His mouth is full," Vasco said through a chuckle, "or he'd tell you he wants to play fetch."

I took the bone and threw it.

The bone carried up and over onto the next level above.

Apparently I'd put some of my frustration into that throw.

I turned to apologize but Magellan was off, speeding away on happy beagle legs.

"If you can reach the top level," Vasco said, "dinner's on me tonight. But only if you don't manage to hit anyone."

Didn't get to try though. Before Magellan was back with the bone,

Janna had rolled up to us, swearing in Orcish. And let me just say that Orcish has some very creative ways to refer to bodily functions, reproductive functions, and ways these things should never be combined.

"Trouble with the Lisatasi?" Vasco asked, voice tense.

"Nothing new," Janna said, frowning so hard I found myself frowning in sympathy.

She took off her thick glasses. Cleaned them on a cloth and put them back on.

"Scott," she said, shaking her head. "If you ever get offered the position of Lord of Portals, don't take it. The perks are nice, but *so* not worth the headaches."

"Don't scare the boy on his first day," Vasco said.

"Wish someone had warned me," Janna grumbled. She sucked in a deep sigh, then blasted it back out and shook her head. "What's up?"

"Tell her what you saw," Vasco said, watching Janna while I recounted everything I'd perceived while viewing the recent history of the Ross Island Portal.

"You think it's Quelan?" Janna said, her eyes still watching me.

"She used Locksmith techniques to open the portal, but Nuastil magic to slam the scrying door on Scott. Who else?"

Janna closed her eyes. Settled back in her wheelchair. She raised her hands, and invisible power buzzed out casting in many directions, all at once.

I yearned to ask what she was doing. Knew I wouldn't be allowed to interrupt with another question.

I turned to Magellan, who'd slipped back quietly. Hoped throwing his bone would distract me, but the bone was gone.

My eyes widened.

Magellan uttered a soft "whuf" that told me he'd gotten his bone and put it away. For now.

Janna's eyes opened. She shook her head.

"Quelan may have passed through, but she couldn't have done anything to put that *riskatan* in the Willamette. If she'd used energies that way, the alerts I'd set up would have informed me, and none of those alerts have been tampered with."

"You know her, I don't," Vasco said. "Any chance she accomplished this without Locksmith skills or Nuastil magic?"

"A sniper with a choice doesn't risk fighting a tiger with a knife."

"Who is this Quelan?" I asked, spitting the words out before anyone could move the conversation along. "And why—"

"Quelan," Janna said, "is the reason only humans have been trained as Locksmiths in the last century. She's an elf — a Nuastil, to be precise — and she started combining Locksmith skills with Nuastil magic in ways that put the entire portal system in jeopardy."

"And she's still alive?" I marveled.

"We don't kill unless forced to," Janna said. "My predecessor closed her mind to Locksmithing, but she somehow reopened it. Some trick combining Nuastil magic and the right location is my best guess."

"But—"

"By the time she recovered, I was the new Lady of Portals." Janna sighed. "She immediately tried setting up a new portal system to help ... certain groups circumvent the restrictions they'd agreed to by treaty."

"Smuggling?" I asked.

"Among other things," Vasco said. "Took all the Locksmiths to root out and shut down the kidnapping ring she'd established."

"Not to mention the cover-up." Janna rubbed her forehead, right above the bridge of her nose. "I closed all earth portals to her for a period of fifty years, in hopes that she would change. And until she demonstrated such change, I barred her permanently from touching power on earth except to travel by portal, and defend herself from threats."

"So that's why you didn't detect her slapping Scott down," Vasco said. "I was afraid she'd figured out a way around your restrictions."

"I wish I could rule that possibility out. She's clever." Janna sighed. "No, you'll have to bring her in."

"I agree," Vasco said, "but still. Track Quelan? Through portals?

Dangerous and time consuming. You can't give this assignment to Scott. It's his first day."

"What if she didn't do it herself?" I asked.

Janna, Vasco, and Magellan all turned to look at me. Only Magellan tilted his head and perked his ears.

"She could be working with someone else." I shook my head. "Look at the timing. She vanishes through *that* portal, close to the time a *riskatan* is found in the Willamette, no more than a few hundred yards away?"

"She'd know we'd check that portal," Janna said.

"And she'd know our first thought would be that she did it," Vasco said. "Found some way around the restrictions. She knows we'd pursue her. We'd have to."

"With her skill at false trails," Janna said, "we'd have to commit multiple Locksmiths to the chase. And an unguessable amount to time."

"And while we chase her," Vasco said, "her partner accomplishes the real goal?"

"Exactly." I jumped to my feet. "They'd assume a little time to organize and get the chase underway. But if I'm right, the partner will make *hris* move soon. There's no time to waste."

"I'll monitor the portals for signs of her return, just in case," Janna said. "What's your next move, Locksmith?"

"I need to cut down variables. I need to talk to that *dorach*."

"Brikatika is his name. He was interviewed yesterday. Just a citizen out for a swim. No politics to him. No reason to target him."

"But why him? Why yesterday? Why that spot?" I shook my head. "This Brikatika knows something. Whether he realizes it or not."

"All right," Vasco said, coming to his feet. "Let's go."

17

DORACHS, OF COURSE, LIVED IN WATER.

My initial thought was that their resemblance to river otters meant they could travel pretty freely along the Willamette, and its shore.

Now that I had a deeper understanding of things, though, I knew that wasn't quite true.

Dorachs looked enough like river otters that everyday people didn't mind seeing them. In fact, since most humans seemed to like otters, there was a better than average chance that humans would want to look at them.

Which was where the problem came in.

Dorachs were too big for river otters. That meant that *dorachs* risked getting their pictures in tabloids, uploaded onto the internet, or even showing up on the news. If they weren't careful.

That could lead to scientists coming to investigate the deviation. It could lead to poachers. Could lead to all sorts of problems.

So *dorachs* had adapted. They'd let themselves play along the water line now and then, but mostly they stuck to diving deeper, and finding or making air pockets for themselves.

Which meant that the local *dorach* community was based in a dug out cavern system under the Willamette.

Which meant that, for the second time in two days, I had to dunk down into the cold, cold waters of the Willamette.

Joy.

No need to change my clothes, though. Oh, no. As soon as Vasco brought us out through the Ross Island Portal and onto that little spike of rocky, dirty shore in the middle of the Willamette River, a spell occurred to me.

Oh, the Locksmiths didn't call them spells. They didn't really talk about Locksmithing as magical at all. They just referred to skills and energies.

I always liked the idea of magic though, so until someone taught me a difference between "magic" and "what Locksmiths do" I was more than content to just consider my new job "magic."

And the spell that occurred to me?

It was a way to stay dry and breathe while underwater.

"Unbelievable," I said, shaking my head.

I was standing at the very tip of the banana stem, there on Toe Island. Vasco was on my right, and Magellan on my left. The sun was still low in the east, over Mount Hood, from this angle, and Portland was just really waking up to its Sunday morning.

"What's unbelievable?" Vasco asked as soon as he'd finished preparing himself and Magellan for our coming dip.

"All morning I've been getting this poor silk shirt soaked by river spray. But that wasn't enough to bring back the memory of this spell."

"Skill," Vasco corrected. "And you're really remembering it now because you'll need to be able to breathe."

He clapped me on the shoulder. "Cheer up. Now that you recall it, it's part of your more active arsenal. Won't happen again."

I gestured to my silk shirt.

Vasco winked. "At least you'll only have to dry-clean it the once."

"There's not a spell for that, is there?"

"Specifically dry cleaning clothing?" Vasco said. "Not a formal Locksmith skill. Now come on."

And we dove into the river.

Didn't feel so shockingly cold this time, but that was likely the effect of the spell. It seemed to be preserving my body heat, even as it allowed me to breathe and...

Wait. I wasn't breathing air from a bubble, the way I expected. Rather, instead, I seemed to have temporary gills on my neck.

And yet, my clothes, so far as I could tell in the water, seemed to stay dry.

Neat effect. I hoped it worked in snowy weather as well.

But now I had to pick up speed to catch up with Vasco and Magellan. They were both jetting along like Olympic athletes.

Even the beagle, which seemed a little unfair. I mean, he was still doing a dogpaddle kind of stroke, but he was keeping pace with Vasco as though he had fins.

Still, I didn't have any trouble catching up to them. So that was some consolation. Might have been that Vasco was so much older than I was.

More likely, he was slowed down by his duffel bag.

I wanted to ask about that, about how Magellan could swim so well, and whether it was something he'd trained at, or an effect created by Vasco.

The problem was that my vocal cords weren't working right. I couldn't produce any sound.

Vasco must have noticed my attempt, though, because he grinned at me.

I'd expected to lose light, as we got deeper under the surface of the Willamette, but the ability to see clearly underwater must have been part of the effect.

Irritating. I could remember the spell I'd just used. The word of power was *xiros*, and the gesture was a quick movement of fins on the side of my head.

But now that I'd already created the effect, the details of how it worked seemed to have become need-to-know. And since it was working, apparently I didn't need to know.

One of these days, I was going to figure out how to trigger these memories at *my* option, not someone else's.

Anyway, fewer fish through this part of the Willamette. Fewer swimming lizardfolk or spirits as well. Might have been the hour. Might have been that this part of the river was more heavily used, and thus more avoided.

Either way, I didn't run across anything that drew my attention before we reached the dug out cave system used by the *dorachs*.

The caves started in the west bank of the Willamette, a hole down where the curve of the bank flatted out into the river bottom.

The sides of the opening cave were a dark gray rock, and I could feel that energies had been applied to keep mud away, as well as to control what came and went through that cavern opening.

It was a ward of some kind. Not Locksmith work, but an innate ability of the *dorachs*. Or perhaps merely something they developed themselves over of the course of their history.

Either way, as we approached, I suddenly knew the gesture needed to open the ward to us.

I didn't hesitate. I went right for it.

Vasco grabbed me by the shoulder. Shook his head.

And let me just say, I thought Vasco's gray hair was long and wild out in the air?

That was nothing to seeing it underwater. His hair went out all directions, like he had a crop of gray seaweed on his head.

I missed his first attempt to tell me, by gesture, why he'd stopped me, because I took one look at his hair and started laughing.

That got me a sour frown that sobered me right up.

Vasco showed me a quick twirl of his fingers that triggered another memory. It was a way of knocking on a ward. Not so much for permission, as to announce through the ward that a Locksmith was about to enter.

Once he'd sent out the right pulse of energy through the right gesture, he nodded his head to me.

I opened the ward to us.

It didn't part or anything. It just went from being a ward that would keep us out to a ward that kept out things and people that weren't us.

Just as well. If the ward had come down, the Willamette would have come in with us. Didn't want to make a mess like that on my first day.

Anyway, I opened the ward to us, and then we were inside a gray stone ... airlock, after a fashion. It was just a little entry chamber, with a single tunnel leading out of it. A tunnel that curved immediately to the north, and looked even tighter than the confines currently surrounding us.

The airlock ceiling was low enough that even Vasco had to duck down. I practically had to crouch. The sides were close enough that with three of us there — even though Magellan was a beagle and thus, pretty small —the entryway felt pretty darn cramped.

The rocky floor was slick and slimy, and smelled like lichen. A strong enough smell to overwhelm even Vasco's animal musk scent. The odor of lichen clung to my tongue.

But though the chamber was wet, I noted that I was dry again.

I do mean dry, too. Head to toe, I was dry as bone. Even my silk shirt had lost its water spots.

Magellan barked and wagged at that sight.

"Thought that might tidy things up for you." Vasco clapped me on the shoulder. Both he and Magellan were as dry as I was. "Neat side effect, if you remember it."

I mumbled to myself what the spell was and what it did, while we stood there. After three repetitions, I turned to Vasco.

"You're the one who's been here before. You lead the way."

"Oh, no," he said, and even Magellan barked a refusal. "Entering this opening is one thing. Barging into the heart of their community is another. Only ever do that if you're pursuing someone who's broken the treaty."

I could remember the *dorach* treaty now. Not a long one. Mostly proscriptions against activities that no decent society wanted to encourage: assault, robbery and the like. It was the kind of treaty that I mentally shorthanded into *don't be a dick and you're welcome here.*

We weren't waiting long. And to my surprise, Brikatika himself came sort of galumphing into the chamber.

Well, not quite *into* the chamber. He stopped in the tunnel, just outside the entry chamber, when he noticed how crowded it was.

I had no trouble recognizing Brikatika, which surprised me a little bit. I mean, before yesterday, all otters looked pretty much alike to me.

Had to have been something in my training. Something that taught me to look for the subtle distinctions in the appearances of nonhumans, to ensure that I didn't mistake one people for another, much less one person for another.

In Brikatika's case, his dorsal coat was dark brown and his ventral coat was closer to cinnamon in shade. But both dorsal and ventral, he had small bands of gray shooting through the main color.

"It's you!" Brikatika said as soon as he saw me. He stood on his back legs and extended his forepaws for me to shake.

That wasn't a *dorach* gesture, which meant he was trying to offer me extra respect by offering me a human gesture of thanks.

I shook his forepaws — both of them, so maybe he didn't understand the gesture as well as he thought, not that I'd point it out to him — and he chattered at me in his native tongue.

"*You saved my life. You saved my wife's mate. You saved my children's father. You saved future generations their progenitor. If ever I or mine may perform you a service, you have only to ask.*"

"*No need for that,*" Vasco said in *dorach*. "*He is a Locksmith.*"

"*He was not when he saved me.*" Brikatika squeezed my hands. "*I insist. Say you will accept this offering of thanks.*"

Formal words. Refusing Brikatika would have caused an incident.

"*Of course I accept,*" I said. "*And may the fortunate timing of our meeting prove a blessing to both our houses.*"

No, I was not planning on saying that. The words just came out. They were the right words, though. Brikatika squeezed my hands once more, and released them.

"*This is formal Locksmith business now,*" Vasco said.

"*Of course. You have new questions?*"

"*I am told,*" I said, "*that you have no role in politics. That you were about no special business yesterday.*"

"*I was not,*" Brikatika said, then recounted a morning as boring as that of any human office worker. The *dorach* equivalent of arising with the alarm clock and settling into an hour of traffic before trudging into work.

At least, if someone randomly tried to kill that office worker, while he poured his first cup of coffee on his way to his desk.

Vasco shrugged at me. It sounded more and more as though this poor *dorach* just happened to be in the wrong place at the right time.

There had to be something though. Something about this *dorach*. I already knew it wasn't about that spot of the Willamette, or even about something else happening during the *riskatan* attack.

Locksmiths had already checked into the obvious possibilities, on the assumption that the attack had been intended as a simultaneous distraction.

Brikatika had to be the answer. But how?

18

VASCO WAS EAGER TO GET OUT OF THIS TIGHT ENTRYWAY TO THE Portland area *dorach* community. He was shifting back and forth with impatience.

Magellan, beside him, had started pawing eagerly at the slick, slimy floor of what I thought of as a cramped little airlock under the Willamette River.

Couldn't blame either of them. The smell of lichen was thick in the air. The walls were close enough that Vasco and I were both inside each other's personal space. I kept bumping his duffel bag.

Not to mention that the ceiling was low enough that he had to duck a bit, and I had to crouch.

What was worse, thought, was now that we'd been inside for a few minutes, I could feel the dampness of the air. Sticking my nice, dark blue silk shirt to my back. Making my jeans cling. And making every breath feel sticky.

But Brikatika remained just inside the tunnel that would lead to the *dorach* caverns proper. Standing on his hand legs, with his body curving forward like a question mark. Whiskers twitching with eagerness to help.

Or maybe eagerness to get back to whatever business I was keeping him from?

That didn't seem too likely. After all, he'd formally offered me a debt, to thank me for saving his life yesterday. He couldn't want to get rid of me. I had to be misinterpreting...

"We should get out of your whiskers," Vasco said, in the chittering *dorach* language. *"Thank you for—"*

"Wait," I said, in the same tongue. My instincts were itching at me. *"Brikatika, have you left the community since yesterday?"*

"No," Brikatika said. *"After the attack, I rushed right here. I have remained within our warded area since."*

"What are you getting at?" Vasco asked, in English. He sounded curious, though, not accusatory.

"I'm not sure," I said. I stopped and shook my head.

I looked over at Brikatika, whose nose twitched as though puzzled at what we were saying. But his whiskers still looked anxious to me.

"Wait," I said, watching Brikatika, but addressing Vasco. "Do *dorachs* speak English?"

"No," Vasco said. "They don't have the vocal..." He turned to look at Brikatika. "They don't have the vocal cords to pronounce English. And since all Locksmiths speak *Dorach* most don't bother learning to understand it."

"I really must get back," Brikatika said. *"My mate will be worrying by now and—"*

"Not so fast," I said.

I met Vasco's eyes.

"You said you heard a cry for help," Vasco said to me. "It didn't occur to me that you heard English."

"But why didn't you—"

"I've been speaking so many languages for so long, I don't always track which one I'm using. Or hearing. Not unless I think about it."

We both turned back to face Brikatika, whose whiskers now twitched with nothing that could be mistaken for impatience.

He was afraid of something.

"Where—" Vasco started, but I cut him off.

Where might have been important. As might how, given the vocal cord issue. But I had a feeling another question was even more critical.

"Why did you learn English?"

Brikatika looked left and right.

"You owe me," I reminded Brikatika, sticking to his own language, even though I knew now that he both spoke and understood English.

Brikatika gave a chittering cry, and the ward behind us collapsed.

The icy waters of the Willamette blasted into us.

I crashed into Vasco, and together we slammed first into the slimy wall of the cavern, and then got carried down into the tunnel. The sides of the tunnel scraped my skin and tore my clothes.

Vasco lost his duffel bag in there somewhere. And I think he lost Magellan too.

I couldn't pay attention to that though. I was too busy trying not to drown. And to protect my head.

Some instinct must have made me squeeze my lips shut as the river waters hit me. And I managed to keep my lips closed through the pressure and all that tossing about.

But I was still getting punched by that sudden water pressure, as well as getting propelled down a tight, tight tunnel.

When the tunnel curved, I hit the wall hard enough to see stars. I tried to grab hold of something. Anything. But it was no good. The walls were rocky enough to hurt, but too slimy for my hands to find any purchase.

All I managed to do was hurt my fingers.

I hit my head on the next pass. Pain jolted my mouth open in an outpuff of breath.

Good news was that my hand was in position to cover my mouth. Gave me the awful, sour taste of lichen, but kept me from immediately sucking in water and drowning.

Bad news was that I was running out of air fast. And I was dazed. Not sure which direction was good. Not sure I could tell one direction from another in the growing darkness.

Not sure I could remember the combination of gesture and incantation that would provide me underwater freedom to breathe and move about as I chose.

I tried. But I kept bouncing off of the sides of the tunnel. Bruising and scraping myself. Tearing my clothes more and more.

My lungs screamed for air. My diaphragm quivered with the need to suck in life-giving oxygen.

It was fully dark now. Everywhere about me. But whether that darkness was from the blow to my head or just how far underground we were now, I had to way to tell.

It was so dark my eyes imagined little flares of light that weren't there.

At least, I don't *think* they were there.

Couldn't focus on that.

Icy waters sapped the energy from my body, as well as the heat.

My body started panicking. All I could do to huddle together in what little warmth I had, and fight to keep from trying to breath.

Suddenly someone grabbed my hand. Had to be Vasco, unless there was another human down here.

Warmth flooded back into me.

Air!

Sweet air. I hadn't opened my mouth, but...

Yes! I had gills again. And the pressure no longer felt as though it were trying to squeeze me flat.

I could kick and swim against that water pressure. And I could see too. The world was a dark blue-green, but I could see as well as I could during a shadowless twilight on the surface world above us.

All around us were more *dorachs*, thoroughly confused about why their home was flooded. Or maybe about why we were there in their homes instead of in the airlock.

But they didn't matter. Brikatika mattered. We needed to find him. Fast.

I looked around at Vasco, who nodded.

And now that I could see better, I realized I could see Magellan paddling through the water next to Vasco.

Knowing he was all right made me feel better. But anger still burned inside me. And not just me. Vasco had that look to his eyes too.

Even Magellan looked pissed. His jaws were set to bare his teeth, and his eyes were narrowed.

And so the three of us swam out of the *dorach* cavern. Though Vasco paused to reset their airlock ward for them.

Just as well. I didn't know how to do it, and it only required a moment.

And then we were swimming. Vasco in the lead, and me right behind.

But we were swimming up.

I lamented my lack of vocal cord access now. I desperately wanted to ask what the hell he was doing. Remind him that we needed to hunt down Brikatika before he got away entirely.

But all I could do was follow Vasco to the surface.

He led me right back to Toe Island, where the dry, rocky surface was suddenly a welcome sight.

The morning sun was blissfully warm.

The three of us flopped down on the rocks. All three, panting for breath. I ached all over. My clothes ruined, and more bruises and scrapes than I could count.

Vasco looked better off, but not by a whole lot. His clothes had handled the rock walls better than mine. He'd definitely gotten his share of bumps and scrapes though.

Magellan seemed to have come through it the best of the three of us. He was first to his feet and growling. Pointing north, as though...

"Can he smell through water?" I asked.

"Yes!" Magellan barked. "Yes I can. I'm the best dog ever. And I'm going to track Brikatika down. And we're going to solve this mystery. And I'm going to get *so many treats.*"

"Yes, you will," Vasco said, "But first, I need a moment to catch my breath. Not as young as I used to be."

"How old ... are you?"

What can I say? The question had been bugging me for some

time now. Especially since Janna implied that she'd served as Lady of Portals for more than fifty years.

I mean, she looked like a teenager to me. She didn't sound like one, true, but she...

"I'm about a hundred and seventy," Vasco said. "Birth records weren't so certain, where I was born. Besides. Truth is, once I became a Locksmith, I stopped keeping track."

"Why?"

"How long will you live?" Vasco asked, and the question triggered the answer inside me.

"Locksmiths stop aging when they gain their mastery. Aging is a function of personal energies, and thus under our control."

"Exactly," Vasco said. "I wasn't young when I gained my power, like Janna."

"But," I said, "if age is a function of personal energy, couldn't you reduce your age?"

"Not sure. Never tried, and I can't think of anyone who has. Might be possible, I suppose." Vasco shrugged. "Nothing wrong with getting old, Scott. Even if you don't do it anymore."

He lay back on the rock, basking in the sun. We were both dry again, at least, but we'd both had quite a shock of cold before he'd managed to get the spell back up for us.

"I enjoyed every stage of my life as I got to it," Vasco said. "Didn't see any reason to go backward now."

"Well," I said, standing up and stretching my aches, "You must admit that your current age does seem to have increased your rest requirements over youth. I'm ready to go."

"So am I, youngster," Vasco said, eyes closed. "But it's not time yet."

"What do you mean? We have to—"

"We have to let Brikatika think he got away. If he thinks he got away, he'll go warn whoever he rushed off to warn. Or he'll get to his hidey-hole, and we'll find him there, instead of forcing him to abandon a place he feels safe and go someplace risky. Like the Columbia."

"Won't he know we can follow him?"

"Doubtful," Vasco said. "Most hounds couldn't track underwater. And most Locksmiths couldn't do it either. Not something as fast as a *dorach* on a mission."

"So how long do we wait?"

"Not long," Vasco said, sitting up and stretching. "Just long enough for me to summon back my duffel bag, and dig us out a little field medicine."

"Ooh," Magellan barked, wagging his tail despite his own impatience to get to the hunt. "I love watching this."

Vasco knelt down, both his bruised and scraped knees on the dry, dirty rocky surface of Toe Island.

He reached his hands down toward the water, but not into it.

I expanded my own awareness. Stretched a part of my mind forward, so that I could track exactly what it was he was...

There.

I hadn't had a chance to really investigate the web of energy structures woven into and around Vasco's duffel bag. But I could tell Vasco had hooked into one of them.

The color of the strands of energy were on the deepest edge of violet. Almost colorless. And working with them emitted a high-pitched whine.

But it wasn't quite a whine. A high-pitched whine like that, I would normally expect it to be a cutting, uncomfortable sound. Something that would make Magellan cringe, and maybe set my teeth on edge.

Like a dentist's drill.

But this whine, it was ... soft. That was the only way I could think of it. Instead of cutting through my head, it just sort of settled around me, while the energies Vasco worked with drew his duffel bag out from somewhere down below, and all the way up to where we waited on the surface.

Then, the duffel burst out of the water, into the air, and landed in Vasco's arms. It looked every bit as dry as we were. Drier, even, because no river spray had hit it yet.

"Again! Again! Again!" Magellan kept barking as he rushed back and forth in front of Vasco.

"Hush," Vasco said. Then turned to me with a smile. He pulled out a small jar, different from the one before.

"This won't feel good," he said, "but it will work quickly."

I gritted my teeth against what was coming.

19

THERE WAS A TIME WHEN I LOVED PISTACHIO ICE CREAM.

It was always my mom's favorite flavor, so every summer we'd have plenty of it around the house. I grew to favor it over even chocolate.

Sacrilege, I know.

But sitting on the back porch on a warm summer evening, eating pistachio ice cream and finding interesting shapes in the shadows of neighborhood trees, that was one of my favorite childhood memories. I used to sit back there with my friends Sean and Darrel and make up stories about the shapes we saw.

Sometimes we even saw strange lights in the sky. We kids were convinced we'd seen UFOs, though my parents always explained those lights away with the most mundane excuses.

Of course, knowing what I know now, I realize we might well have seen UFOs. Or at least, I might have, and made Sean and Darrel see them once I pointed them out.

All those happy memories, all tied to the taste of pistachio ice cream.

And all of them, *ruined* by a little alchemical concoction called Bruisebane.

Looked like some kind of nutmeg paste, but it smelled like pistachios. And worse than that, when it was rubbed into cuts and bruises, I got the taste of pistachio ice cream on my tongue.

All of that might have been fine.

But Bruisebane hurt like hell.

Vasco and I stood there on the northern tip of Toe Island. Cool river spray on the breeze. Boats darting here and there along the Willamette, though no one paid us any special attention.

That had to do with something Vasco had done. I didn't catch just what. But there was enough of a supernatural kick to it that most folks would turn away from us.

I think he did it because there was no way we wouldn't stand out now. Two men and a beagle, standing on a rock in the river, with no boat to have gotten them there?

Plus, Vasco and I both had to strip down to apply the Bruisebane to ourselves.

Two men in their undies, on that rock in the river? No way anyone would miss it. Especially since we didn't even have pre-dawn gloom to help us now.

The sun was fully up, but its warmth just made the chill of the river spray more noticeable. Or maybe it was just that I was more aware of my skin. I was covered in cuts and bruises, from getting slammed around the entryway and then the tunnel leading into the *dorach* community.

My nice twilight blue silk, torn in at least a dozen places, and still covered in a residue of slimy lichen. My blue jeans had fared better, but even they were torn in a couple of spots, and just as covered in lichen residue.

Both my shirt and jeans were dry, at least, but there wasn't a dry cleaner in the world who could get that much lichen out of silk. Not to mention the numerous tears.

But all of that was only in the back of my mind. In the front of my mind were all the cuts and bruises I'd sustained while my clothes were getting damaged.

Now that I'd had a few minutes of rest on that rock, all those little wounds had started stiffening up.

This was why the Bruisebane was so important. I had to be healed *now*. I had to be ready to jump back into the river and go after Brikatika, and I mean ASAP.

I kept telling myself that as I applied the horrible stuff.

How to describe it...

Everywhere I applied the Bruisebane, it felt as though the cut or bruise was being pulled slowly out of my body.

Yes, healthy flesh was left behind. But the pulling process was excruciating.

I'd like to think I didn't make any sounds less manly than a growl through gritted teeth.

In my more honest moments, I'm fully aware that growls can rarely be confused with whimpers.

By the time I was done, my whole body was ringing. Trembling. I felt healthy and strong, but the sudden absence of all that pain jarred me. Left me standing there, shaking my head. Trying to get the taste of pistachio ice cream off my tongue.

And I wasn't going to have any luck on that score. That taste *lingered*.

Finally, the shaking diminished. The ringing sensation too.

Finally I could hear something more than the sound of my own rushing blood. Feel more than the pounding of my heart.

Yes, all the hair on my head — and everywhere else on my body — was matted down with sweat. But I was ready to go.

Except for one thing.

"Mind putting your clothes back on?" I tried to ignore the humor in Vasco's voice as I turned to the...

...pile of clothes? I was pretty sure I'd torn off my jeans and silk shirt at speed, eager to get the Bruisebane experience over with. And yet, they were folded neater than I'd do myself after taking them out of the laundry.

And the tears and rips were gone.

So was the lichen.

Even my shoes and socks looked pristine.

"Okay," I said, as I stuffed my feet back into my pants. "How did you do that? Because there's nothing in my arsenal coming to mind. And I'm pretty sure I had cause for any relevant memories to surface."

"You're a Lock*smith*," Vasco said, sounding thoroughly pleased with himself. "I'm the Lock*master*. My ring has a few more keys on it than yours."

We both reflexively chuckled at the "keys" reference, while I dressed at record speed. I found a small double-sided container of Serpent's Kiss and Bruisebane.

Clearly intended to be my emergency stash until I had a chance to make some of my own.

I turned around, and Vasco looked ready to go. Even had his wild gray hair tied back with a leather thong. Made the lines of his face more visible, but it made him look less homeless and more badass. Like he was an original member of the Navy's WWII Underwater Demolition Team.

Except, of course, he was way too old for that.

He also didn't look as sweaty and stressed out from the Bruise-bane as I did, which was just not fair.

I'd never point it out though. Not after the age discussion we'd just had. And from the twinkle in his eye, he was expecting it. So I looked at Magellan instead.

Magellan, he looked eager to go too. Padding back and forth on the rock, with his nose turned north and an impatient little whine coming out of him.

"So," I said. "How do we do this?"

"With a speed boost, of course."

Speed boost. Those two words hit me like a thunderbolt. And just like that, the memory of what that was and how it worked leapt back into my head.

The power word was *tachytita*. The gesture was a slap to both heels.

And after I did that, I could outrun the wind and outswim damn near anything.

Vasco used a similar technique to include Magellan, but I didn't recognize it. Either it was a *Lockmaster* thing, or it was need-to-know, and I didn't.

I didn't care though. The chase was what mattered.

I repeated the underwater freedom spell — skill, whatever — and I was good to go.

Just like that, we were off.

Magellan hit the water first, followed by Vasco and myself, just behind him.

Magellan went deep, right down along the floor of the riverbed. Vasco and I flanked him, just behind his tail.

And we tore through that water at speeds that would have made a jet ski jealous.

I'd expected us to kick up tons of river mud into silt behind us, clouding our passage. But we weren't. Just an aspect of the speed boost, or so it seemed.

Not that I could ask Vasco. After all, I had no more voice now than I did the last two times I'd used the underwater freedom spell.

We outswam fish. We outswam boats. We outswam even the fastest of the lizardfolk sharing the river with us.

Vasco's duffel bag didn't seem to slow him in the least.

And Magellan, he seemed to know right where he was going. He swept us back and forth across the riverbed. Up at times, down at times, and every movement likely to mirror exactly the movements that Brikatika had done only a few minutes before.

Exactly how long before? That I wasn't sure, but I knew a quarter hour hadn't passed.

At this speed, the river felt less like water than gelatin, except that it was gelatin that responded to us. Every kick of my feet, every sweep of my hands, the gelatinous water just flew behind me.

I found myself wondering just how far Brikatika could have gotten. But just as the question occurred to me, Magellan slowed down. Then he circled in the water.

We were somewhere along the Multnomah Channel by now. I didn't know the area well enough to know just where, but I did know a full minute hadn't passed since we went through the ward that would have kept out *riskatani*.

The river was narrower here, but a little deeper. And by now, the fish, eels, spirits and lizardfolk were giving us a wide berth.

Vasco's full attention was on Magellan. Magellan wasn't barking, but I felt sure he was communicating with Vasco through a series of tail lashes and ear flicks.

Finally, Vasco nodded. Turned to me. Pointed at his eyes with two fingers, then pointed down with one.

I nodded. Expanded my awareness, and swept it down along the riverbed.

Didn't take long. Under the river mud, I could sense a particular rock that had been worked over with energies. No wider than my arm was long, this rock. It was round, and had veins of copper running through it, which meant that it wasn't part of the usual river rocks.

Far as I knew, no one was mining copper in the Willamette.

The web of energies in that rock were tied into something below it.

No. That's not right. Something ... *inside* it. There was a sense of depth to that rock, that had fooled me for a moment.

I turned a puzzled expression on Vasco, but he only firmed his mouth and nodded.

I shrugged.

That was where we were going then.

It wasn't a portal. Not properly speaking. And it wasn't anything that was supposed to be there. It was...

A smile lit me from the inside.

I grabbed Vasco by the shoulder.

Got a puzzled frown for my trouble. I mimed hefting the rock, then pointed back upwards toward the shoreline. After all, it wasn't more than a couple of feet across. And we were underwater. That would help make it more mobile. Or would, at least, once we got it going.

Vasco shook his head.

I nodded firmly and repeated the gesture.

Vasco sighed, but nodded. He waved a hand for me to proceed.

I swam down to the rock, Vasco by my side and Magellan circling us.

I grabbed one edge of the rock. Vasco shook his head, but grabbed the other.

We heaved. Our shoes sank into the riverbed until they hit more rock below.

The rock didn't budge.

Vasco gave me a very clear *satisfied?* look. I frowned, but nodded.

Together we went over the energies, checking for threats.

I found an explosive trigger. It felt like a hot piece of wire. Disarming it meant unwinding it, slowly, from its anchors into the copper of the rock.

Took a few minutes, but I got it done. While I did, Vasco undid a couple of other traps I didn't have time to check out.

I ran through all my senses, and realized I could hear a separate trap. A faint electric buzzing, that I had to counter by focusing on the pitch. Digging into the tone of it.

Then I shifted it up a fifth and it dispersed with the current.

Finally, I nodded at Vasco. I didn't notice anything else, so I figured we were good to go.

Vasco shook his head. Nodded to Magellan.

Magellan swam in close. Sniffed all over.

Pointed with his nose at a spot near the center, and stayed fixed in that position, adjusting his point as necessary against the current of the river.

Me, I was still just as impressed that Vasco could dogpaddle in place under the surface of a river. But then, the underwater freedom spell probably helped with that.

I focused in more intently on the spot Magellan picked out.

Strained my senses.

Sure enough. Something.

I could barely pick out the smell over the pistachio still coating my tongue, but there was a hint of brass polish.

Once I could smell it, I could see it.

The trigger looked like a tiny splinter of energy the color of tarnished copper. Placed right at the spot where I would have to touch it, if I used Locksmith skills to open the passage leading inside.

Unnoticed, it would have hit me with enough explosive power to scatter parts of me all the way to Newport.

Noticed, the splinter required patience and a steady hand to extract. Fortunately, training had given me both.

Then I opened the passage into the rock, and in I went, Vasco and Magellan right behind me.

20

When I triggered the opening sequence of that copper veined rock in the bed of the Multnomah Channel, I'd expected it to open like a portal.

The rock was round, and about as wide as one of my arms, so I'd expected its face to be replaced by a whorl of energy, whose feel and scent would tell me something about its character and destination.

True, I was well underwater at the time, but with the underwater freedom spell — or skill, as Vasco would have me call it — my senses were working pretty well. Everything except my vocal cords.

Yes, I know that my vocal cords aren't a sense. But they were the only part of me not working normally, all right? I think it was a side effect of having gills so close to them. But that's speculation on my part.

Anyway, I'd been expecting the swirling energies, ready to convey me not to some other location or plane of existence, but to some energetically designed interior. Fabricated and manipulated space, built into the rock.

More important than that, I'd been expecting a choice about *when* I went inside.

Most important of all, I wanted to have some idea of what would be waiting for me on the other side *before* I entered.

I mean, I knew I was going to go in. Vasco, Magellan and I got there following Brikatika, which meant that Brikatika had gone into the rock.

And where that *dorach* went, I needed to go.

Still, as a Locksmith, figuring out what's on the other side of portals — and things like portals, into which category this rock fell — was stock in trade. I didn't even have to *try* to have a number of appropriate skills leap back to mind.

I just wanted a moment to prepare before I ventured inside a rock.

(A concept I tried *very hard* not to think too much about at the time, I can tell you.)

The rock didn't work like a portal though.

I triggered the opening.

Icy blue energies swirled around me with the smell of lutefisk.

The rock sucked me right inside.

The world about me now was ice.

The floor was white ice. The walls a pale blue. The ceiling, a dark blue. All of it smelled cold and vaguely like the Willamette River.

But I wasn't freezing.

I mean, my first thought, once my eyes successfully resolved that I was standing in a room made entirely of ice, was that I'd need to huddle in on myself and conserve warmth.

Well, also that I had to hope some personal warmth spell occurred to me before I froze to death.

But I really wasn't that cold. More like forty-degree-day cold, not Jesus-Christ-it-must-be-zero-Kelvin cold.

So after a brief shiver, I settled down and reviewed my surroundings.

The room I stood in had a fifteen foot ceiling, and walls at least twice that far apart. It was longer than it was wide, too. Maybe ... forty feet long?

Something like that.

No furniture in here. No light source either, except maybe the walls.

Yes. Now that I could take a closer look, I could see that the walls were actually the darker blue of the ceiling, except that light emitted from them, lightening their shade and keeping me from being totally blind.

In the wall behind me, I could spot grooves in the shape of a doorway. Not a small, round doorway, but a regular doorway, like the ones in my apartment. No handle, but that didn't worry me.

That door was probably the way back out. But what about the way...

Wait.

Where were Vasco and Magellan?

They'd been right behind me, in the river. When I triggered the rock's opening, they'd been moving forward, same as me.

But they weren't here.

"Great," I muttered aloud. "Looks like there was one more trap."

That brought a snickering laugh that slithered through the air, rather than echoed.

"Yessss...."

I was just about to reply, when the voice continued.

"You arrrre trapped here, Lockssssssmith. Even yourrrr ssssskills cannot open that doorrrr from the inssssside."

Something was wrong with this. And not just the sibilance.

"All right," I said, stretching my senses to try to pick up where that voice came from. "I'm here. And clearly I missed the all-you-can-eat lutefisk lunch. So why don't you tell me where I can find Brikatika."

"Dead."

The word didn't hiss, but it felt as though it should have.

"Sssssorry, Locksssssmith, but you'rre too late to ssssave the *dorach*."

"So, you're confessing to a Locksmith that you violated a treaty? I mean, I haven't met you yet, so I don't know which treaty applies, but I'm pretty sure every treaty we have makes killing a no-no."

My senses were settling in now. I could pick up the energetic patterns that formed the icy structure surrounding me.

It was consistent with the color of the ceiling, and the smell of lutefisk. But there was something off about the sound of it. The energies of this place hissed, when there should have been a slower cycle to them. Should have been something more like a hum.

But what did that mean?

"Funny," the voice said. "You sssssslew a *risssssskatan* with yourrrr own hand."

"I was saving a life." I started slowly through the room, my hands out and moving to keep my awareness going as many directions as possible. "You shouldn't try to pretend you were doing the same thing."

Hissing. I was pretty sure it was laughter.

Something nipped at my ankle. A sudden, icy pain shot up my leg all the way to the knee.

I stumbled. Caught myself on my hands.

More hissing laughter.

"Poorrrr Locksssssmith. Cannot ssssssave the *dorach*. Cannot sssssave himssssssself."

Movement. I could feel it nearby. But the icy pain made my leg throb. Numbness followed the throb, and that numbness started creeping up my calf.

"No," I said. "I can save myself just fine."

Movement to my left. I clenched my arms. Made myself not twitch. Not give away anything.

"I'm a Locksmith. There's a reason we're the badasses of this world."

"Badasssssessss." More snickering, slithering laughter. "Not forrrr long."

"Now just hold on a second. Look. Hissing esses is one thing. Sounds menacing. But what's the deal with your r's?"

Sudden darting in from my left. Coming down from the ceiling.

Looked like a blue-green tentacle, but slimy.

I caught it. Snagged it in both hands.

Not a tentacle. A snake of some kind. Its hood flared out. Its mouth opened wide, fangs dripping purple venom.

It hissed, and that venom got airborne in a cloud of purple gas.

I had to throw the snake away and dive for the floor. Roll along the ice.

I'd evaded the poison cloud. But the snake was gone again.

"All right," I said, coming to my knees. Listing slightly to my left and worrying about the numbness that was reaching my left thigh.

"All right," I said, again. "I know what you look like now, ice serpent. You won't surprise me again. Just give me Brikatika, and maybe I'll let you live. I mean, you attacked a Locksmith, but still, maybe I could make the case that you were defending your home."

Hissing sound. I kept talking.

"But defending your home *and* either harboring or murdering a fugitive from treaty justice?" I shook my head as I turned to try to watch all directions at once. "Can't make that sound like anything other than what it is."

Movement. Behind me.

I flung myself forward. Left leg gave out mid-effort. I banged my head on the ice, but still rolled to my back. My hands came up.

I caught the snake again. This time by the crest. Wrestled with it.

The ice snake's jaws opened wide. Dripped purple venom on my nice silk shirt, and where the venom touched, little spots on my chest went numb.

But no poison cloud this time. I'd guessed right. It couldn't breath the cloud without flaring its hood.

And I had the hood pinned.

"I can snap you," I said. I wasn't sure of that, but it sounded good. And besides, I was a strong guy even before I went through the combat training.

"I mean it," I said. "I'll snap you right here. Rip your head off."

The snake lifted me right off the ground.

The thing had to have been anchored in the ceiling.

There. I could see now where it had a hole it was coming out of.

A hole.

It was attacking me out of a hole.

A hole that hadn't been there earlier. I knew that, because I'd looked. The ceiling had been solid.

"Last chance," I said, confidence all through my voice now. So much confidence that I swear I felt that ice snake hesitate. "I don't want to kill you, but I will."

The ice snake hissed and yanked faster. Maybe it sensed that something was wrong.

Clearly, the snake didn't understand the dual nature of a Locksmith.

Yes, we can open damn near anything.

But we can close damn near anything too.

I tapped into the flow of the icy blue energies of that ceiling.

I slammed the hole shut.

Cut the snake right in half. The half outside the hole fell to the floor.

The snake wasn't dead yet. That astounded me, but even being astounded didn't slow me down. Not now.

The remainder of the snake's body writhed, venting acidic purple ichor all over the left side of the chamber, eating away slowly at the interior.

The head kept trying to bite me.

I slammed its fangs down against the ice of the floor.

Twice.

Three times.

On the fourth repetition, the fangs broke. And that wasn't all. I'd been slamming the thing down with all the force I could muster, which was considerable. When the fangs broke, the jaw unhinged and tore away.

I jumped back, but all the fight had gone out of the snake now. Even the flow of its purple ichor had diminished to a trickle.

The snake twitched a few more times, then was still.

But it occurred to me that one snake hole might hide more than one snake.

I needed to get out of here.

But first, I needed to do something about this spreading numbness, which was now getting dangerously close to, well, let's just say to the top of my thigh.

I hopped over to a corner of the room, well away from the hole, the door in, and most important, the dead snake and the havoc its blood had caused.

Double-puncture wound at my left ankle, with purple lines coming out of it. Already the ankle was swollen. I just hadn't noticed, through the numbness.

Not good.

Worse than that, I could feel my pulse beginning to slow. Get a little thready. That was even less good, especially after a fight.

I was starting to get lightheaded too. The ice chamber got brighter. Not much, but enough to worry me.

I didn't have Vasco's bag of tricks to help me now. Fortunately, the right information came back, as soon as the need was there.

First, I applied Serpent's Kiss to the snake bite.

Felt like I'd shoved hot coals onto the wound.

And I have to admit, on the one hand, that was good. I could feel the burn. Picked my heart rate right back up too, and helped me focus.

Also on the good side, there were no witnesses to the bout of swearing that came out of me then. I must have run through curse words in at least a dozen languages. I know I pounded a few cracks into the ice, too.

But I had more to do. The Serpent's Kiss wasn't enough.

I really didn't want to do this next step.

I stretched my awareness down inside the Serpent's Kiss, where I'd rubbed it into the wound.

I found the energies at the core of the concoction.

And I started dragging those energies up through my leg.

Felt as though I were willingly yanking a downed power line right up my calf and well into my thigh. My free hand kept pounding on the ground. I had my eyes squeezed tight. Drenched myself in sweat. All the muscles in my shoulders and back seized up.

I clenched my teeth so tight I'm amazed they didn't crack.

But it worked.

My leg healed. And I just had to sit there, shivering against the gelling sweat all over my body, while I recovered from the healing, as well as the attack.

Finally, though, I needed to find my way out.

21

SHIVERING ALL ALONE IN A ROOM MADE OF ICE.

As if my first day as a Locksmith weren't weird enough.

Checking portals, checking wards, that had all seemed natural. Part of the job.

Interviewing a potential victim? Brikatika, the *dorach* who'd been attacked by that *riskatan*? Made sense to me.

Been the right move, too. I'd gotten information the first interviewing Locksmiths had missed — Brikatika was hiding something. Something worth throwing his whole community into disarray — not to mention trying to kill three Locksmiths (I'm including Magellan) — and fleeing the scene, before I could find out what.

But now fighting and killing an ice serpent? Torturing myself to heal the damage from its frozen bite?

Those were the kind of experiences they'd left off the Locksmith brochure for a reason.

Still, I'd dallied long enough in recovering.

I stood up. My leg took my weight just fine. A little shaky, maybe, but that was just the aftermath. It would fade soon. The same way the chill of my gelled sweat faded.

Wait. I wasn't really chilly at all now, in this room made of ice. Why was...

As soon as the question occurred to me, the answer came hot on its heels.

Locksmiths tolerate temperature changes beyond anything a normal person could handle. This ability aids Locksmiths in traveling wherever they need to, to tend their duties.

Explained why I hadn't frozen to death yet.

I still needed to figure out where to go next. I had to find Brikatika.

For that matter, I had to find Vasco and Magellan. Make sure they were all right. They were supposed to follow me in here.

Maybe I should go back out the entrance? See if something had prevented them from following?

I did know right where the door was...

No. That felt like the wrong move.

Back would hold no answers for me. No, if Magellan had been right, and I had no reason to doubt the amazing beagle's nose, then Brikatika *had* come this way

And if the *dorach* had passed through here, then there had to be another exit to this ice room.

Yes. That made sense to me. It wasn't that this room was a trap. It was that the ice snake was a threshold guardian, of a sort.

Besides, the chamber might only hold one at a time. Vasco and Magellan might not be able to enter until I left.

That wasn't just a guess. A quick assessment of the energetic patterns of this constructed space indicated that the entrance might only admit one. For assessment, and to control the speed of admittance deeper inside.

So I had to skip the easy solution. What a shock.

I stood in the center of the chamber and stretched forth my awareness again. Not in all directions this time, as when I'd been fighting the ice snake, but in a single direction at a time.

I covered the pale blue walls first, but found nothing there but the door I'd already known about.

I tried the dark blue ceiling next, going over it inch by inch.

I found the hole that the ice snake had come out of.

Paranoia made me follow it. Send my awareness up into the hole and track all the way to the snake's lair. Just in case it had a mate. Or maybe a dozen hungry siblings, all getting ready to come feast on unprepared Locksmith.

The den was another dozen or so feet into the ceiling, right up close to an energetic edge of this constructed space, deep inside the copper-veined rock, which I knew was still resting at the bottom of the Multnomah Channel.

No eggs in the den. No siblings, or mate, either. In fact, there wasn't much there, except...

Well...

Inside the little lair, there was a smooth patch of ice some eighteen inches long and twelve inches high. It served as a television set and, well...

It was tuned to a soap opera. *Dark Shadows*, I think.

I yanked my awareness back. I didn't need to think about the hobbies of the ice snake that had just tried to kill me. The snake that had made me kill it.

Yes, I was defending myself. Yes, it was the only way to stop the thing. Yes, I'd even warned it.

But I'd killed it. And I hated that.

But I didn't have time to wallow right now.

Back to my search.

Nothing else to find on the ceiling, so I turned my attention to the white ice floor. Beginning at the entry, I swept my way across the floor inch by inch.

The places where the ice snake's acidic ichor struck tasted like sour limes through my extended awareness. Sadly, the taste was a pleasant change from the lingering pistachio in my mouth — a taste I'd once loved, but ruined for me forever by the awful experience of the Bruisebane.

Locksmith field healing sucked.

Anyway, tucked away in the far right-hand corner of the room, I found the exit. A trap door, only just wide enough to admit my shoulders.

Checking it for secondary traps burned time I wasn't sure I had, but the last thing I wanted was to get past the guardian, and then get killed by a poison needle or something.

Nothing there. Apparently whoever built this figured the guardian would be enough.

I ripped open the trap door. Dropped feet first down a long, spiraling ice chute.

I'm not proud of what I did then. But I just couldn't help it.

"WHEE!"

What can I say? It was a better ride than any theme park I could name.

A dampener at the exit killed my nearly lethal speed, and dropped me onto a wooden floor...

...in the middle of a very bad situation.

The room was maybe thirty by thirty, all made from dark woods, and lit by torches that put out a yellowish light and smelled like day-old fireworks.

One door in the center of each wall. Three chutes across the ceiling above me.

Vasco to my left. Maybe a dozen paces. Standing under a different chute than I was. He'd lost the leather thong tying back his gray hair, but it looked more matted down with sweat than wild right now.

Vasco bled from wounds on his chest and arms. He held a fighter's crouch, glaring at the bad guys.

Six bad guys. Each of them stood a head taller than me, and easily twice as broad.

They were also covered entirely in long red fur. Hid all the features of their faces, except their yellow eyes and fangs. Did nothing to hide their dirty yellow claws, either. And both their hands and feet had claws.

Information leapt to mind as I saw them.

They were known as *gossaks*. Not much in the way of brains, but a reputation for viciousness that made them popular as henchmen, in certain circles.

Or hench-somethings anyway. They had no gender, and no one knew how they reproduced.

Anyway, they weren't supposed to be in this world at all, because they weren't part of any treaty. The problem in keeping them out was that they could travel across worlds at the sites of messy murders.

With the information came differentiation. I could now see smaller strains of darker fur that created patterns. Allowed me to tell one *gossak* from the other, and remember them later. Every bit as distinctive as facial features, eye and hair color. Which also meant they could be disguised, but few things in life were perfect.

Like this situation.

Vasco already bleeding.

Three of the *gossaks* holding captives. One gripped Magellan with both hands. But it looked as though the little beagle had done some damage of his own first. That *gossak* was bleeding at the leg. Thick, yellowish blood. I might have mistaken it for pus, if I hadn't known better.

Another *gossak* held Brikatika, and the grip looked every bit as threatening as the grip on Magellan. Holding by the scruff and the throat, which would have been bad enough if Brikatika had been the size of a normal otter. Big as he was, he had to be in agony.

That *gossak* looked uninjured.

A third *gossak* held Vasco's duffel bag in one hand. It was shaking the other hand as though stung. And I'm not surprised. That hand was swelling up to at least two or three times its normal size.

The three other *gossaks* looked uninjured — at a glance, anyway — and had formed a half-circle about a dozen feet from Vasco.

The moment I landed, one of the *gossaks* spun to face me, while the other two stayed watching Vasco.

"Whoa," I said, hands coming up and a smile forced across my lips. "Everybody just slow down here."

"*They want to kill me!*" Brikatika yelled in his native tongue, his voice strained. "*Save me, Locksmith!*"

"Everybody calm down," I said, holding that smile for dear life. "Seems to me there's been a misunderstanding."

"Simple choice," the *gossak* facing me said. "Leave or die. We give your boss here same choice."

"Well, you're also holding his best friend, and his duffel bag. So he might be a bit put out—"

"He attacked us."

"Now, just let me guess," I said. "He said you weren't allowed on earth without a treaty, and when you objected he forced the issue?"

No answer but narrowed eyes. Probably not how it played out, but I wanted the try to get the *gossaks* listening to me. And painting the situation in terms that favored them would help. If they bought it.

"So you were just defending yourself then."

Magellan barked an objection, but I waved my hand to still him.

"Look," I said. "It's an easy mistake to make. Vasco and I, we entered this artificial space inside a rock in the Multnomah Channel. Which is on earth. So finding you here, it feels a lot like finding you on earth."

The big one facing me — might not have been bigger than his partners, but facing me made him look bigger — opened his mouth to speak, so I pushed ahead before he could.

"*The mistake there*," I said, "is that you aren't on earth. You're in a rock. Now, for all I know, officially, you guys entered this rock on some other world, and then someone dragged it to earth. Not your fault you ended up here."

"That's right," the one facing me said, and the others nodded quickly.

Too quickly. They were all lying. But that didn't matter right now.

"So you're not in violation of anything, so long as you stay in the rock. And I have no reason to think you'll leave. Right?"

They nodded.

Magellan growled, and I had to wave him to silence again.

"Now. You hurt a Lockmaster, but you were defending yourselves. So I think we can let that go. If—" I held up my pointing finger —

"you release Magellan, the beagle, and give Vasco back his duffel bag."

"It stung me!" the one holding it cried out.

"Well, you shouldn't have tried to search a Lockmaster's bag. Bad policy. Be glad that's all that happened."

That got me some grumbling I didn't like, followed by a whuffed conversation too quick for me to follow.

"We release dog and duffel bag and you leave?"

I really wanted to lie right then, but I knew that would be a mistake.

"You release dog and duffel bag, and you won't get in trouble for hurting Vasco or Magellan. Then if you give us the *dorach*, we'll leave in peace."

"*Dorach* stays," the *gossak* facing me said. "Owes us."

"I'm afraid I have to insist. Brikatika is a material witness in a case I'm investigating."

"*Dorach* stays."

"Then we have a problem," Vasco said, as though he were worried about what I'd say next.

"Look," I said, smiling again. "It's hard to come to terms when a couple of you are hurting. I get that."

I dug around in my pocket, giving Vasco a wink at an angle so the *gossaks* couldn't see my eye.

I pulled out my double-sided jar of Bruisebane and Serpent's Kiss.

"How about I heal that bite wound?"

22

TACTICALLY SPEAKING, THIS SITUATION WAS A MESS.

First of all, not a lot of room to fight. The wooden room was maybe thirty feet to a side. Might have seemed like a lot of room, except that a lot of it seemed to be filled with bad guys.

Six of them, to be specific. Big, red, furry bad guys, with dirty yellow claws on their hands and feet. *Gossaks*, a species with a reputation for viciousness.

That they filled the room with the smell of wet animal did nothing to make me think better of them.

True, two of them had been injured, that I could see. One was bleeding from a beagle bite on its leg — I refuse to give these things the dignity of *hris* as a pronoun — and another's hand had swollen up to three times its normal size, thanks to a sting from something in Vasco's duffel bag.

Unfortunately, one of those *gossaks* held Magellan in a grip that looked as though it was one bad thought away from a dead beagle.

Anther *gossak* still had a good grip on that duffel bag, which was good and bad. Good in that its unstung hand was busy. Bad in that Vasco didn't have access to his bag of tricks.

And one of the other *gossaks* held Brikatika in a tight grip up by the throat. Not much better a position to be in than Magellan's.

Vasco was with me, but he was bleeding from several wounds to his chest and arms. He'd definitely looked better. And he might not have seen the wink I'd tried to shoot him.

I could only hope he did.

So I faced those six sets of suspicious, yellow eyes, and held up my little double-sided jar of Bruisebane and Serpent's Kiss.

And I smiled with a lot more sincerity than I'd managed earlier.

"This," I said, hefting the jar, "is how I survived a bit from the ice serpent you had stationed as a threshold guardian."

That got them whuffing back and forth at each other in tones I couldn't quite pick out.

I might or might not have recognized their language. Tough to be sure because they spoke a pidgin version of something to each other, and they did it fast and slurred.

"Show," the one closest to me said.

I tugged up the left leg of my blue jeans. Showed the healing, almost gone bite marks, and the twin holes in the jeans.

"This will heal the dog bite too?"

"Sure will," I said, and Magellan growled an objection to my healing his captor. I nodded at him, and hoped the *gossaks* didn't speak Beagle.

"Give," the closest *gossak* to me said, one hand forward.

"No way," I said, shaking my head slowly. "This stuff is the most valuable thing I have, and you'd use way too much. I'll apply it myself."

"Trick."

"How could healing you be a trick? Don't you know Locksmiths don't slow down for anything?" — I knew that was our reputation — "This stuff is how we do it."

And I had complete honesty in my voice as I said that.

I think the honesty of my tone did me as much good as my words.

But then, they had no way of knowing how much Bruisebane and Serpent's Kiss hurt while they worked.

I picked my cautious way across the floor to the one who held Magellan.

"You should put down the dog," I said. "If this stuff relaxes you wrong, he could bite you."

Another *gossak* stepped over to take the hostage, and I stood up straight.

"Just a damned minute. I'm over here offering to heal one of you. The least you can do is let my friend's dog go."

"Dog bit me."

"And your claws are hurting him. I'd say you're even. Plus, I'm about to heal the bite."

I stared right back into those yellow eyes. I saw no sign of yielding.

"Let the dog go, or no healing for you. I can demonstrate my good will on our friend with the bad hand instead."

"Me!" the *gossak* with the stung, swollen clawed hand said. "Me!"

"No!" the bitten *gossak* said. "Me."

And he released Magellan, who winced, but trotted somewhere behind me.

"Now hold still," I said, scooping out some Serpent's Kiss on one finger. Too little to really heal that bite, but that was fine with me.

I made a show of taking a deep breath.

"Now," I said, "this might sting a little, at first. So I want you to count to three for me, and I'll apply the ointment on three."

That got me suspicious eyes again, so I pointed to my healed ankle.

"One," the *gossak* said.

I put away the jar.

"Two."

I positioned myself so my finger was right above the bite wound, which was still dripping thick, smelly yellow blood.

"Three."

A lot of things happened at the same time.

I slapped a fingerful of Serpent's Kiss on the wound.

The *gossak* screamed as the fiery healing began.

Magellan leapt right for the throat the *gossak* holding Brikatika.

Vasco crippled a *gossak* that it turned out he'd already hurt, before I'd entered the room.

I immediately brought my right fist up with all my strength — amplified with Locksmith training and skills as well as using everything my body could give me.

I slammed that *gossak's* jaw for all I was worth.

I saw the huge thing's clawed feet leave the floor, but I didn't stick around to see the results. I spun—

—right into Vasco's duffel bag, swung by the stung *gossak*.

The bag hit me, but it wasn't hard enough to hurt. Instead it slammed me into a furry wall — the *gossak* I'd just punched.

I took the opportunity to give that *gossak* another crack, using the back of my head against its jaw.

As I pulled away, I heard the *gossak* behind me slump to the floor.

The stung *gossak* threw aside the duffel now. Approached with its good hand high and menacing.

But whatever had given the *gossak* that sting had slowed it down.

I waited for it to come in at me with that claw. It came in high.

I ducked under the blow. Danced to the *gossak's* right and brought the knife-edge of both hands into the *gossak's* stung hand, one strike to each side.

It screamed. Threw itself at me.

I ducked. Grabbed that swollen hand and twisted. Flipped the *gossak* through the air and into the wooden wall.

The wood must have been façade. Because the *gossak* hit with a dull thump, as though it had slammed into stone.

The stung hand ended up near the floor.

I brought down an axe kick on that poor, swollen clawed hand, with all the focus I could muster.

Bones broke, and something unhealthy squished. Broke the surface of the *gossak's* skin.

Something foul, odorous and black seeped out.

The *gossak* screamed again and passed out from the pain.

I spun to see what was going on in the rest of the room.

Vasco had taken down one *gossak*. He was in close and mixing it up with another. Throwing punches but taking too many claws.

He was getting woozy. His punches weaker.

Magellan and Brikatika had taken down one *gossak*, and were squaring off with another. Magellan tried to harry it, but Brikatika had only an otter's grace on land. Not nearly enough for pack fighting.

"Help Vasco!" I yelled at Magellan.

Magellan darted toward his friend.

That was a mistake, on my part.

I'd thought my voice would be enough to turn the *gossak* from the *dorach*, which wasn't much of a threat, to face me. A Locksmith. A much greater threat.

But the *gossak* had already chosen its target. Grabbed up Brikatika in both claws. Ready to rip the *dorach* in half.

I had only moments to stop that *gossak*.

Which meant I had only one option.

In regular martial arts, flying kicks are a showy thing. Useless in a real fight. Too slow to be effective, and they tended to make the kicker an easy target.

However.

Locksmith martial arts applied energies in creative ways.

So when I roared, charged, and leapt into the air, I wasn't just leaping into a kick.

I was lassoing the *gossak* with energies. Energies that accelerated me beyond anything short of jet speed. Drew the blade of my kicking foot right into the join of the *gossak's* head with its neck.

The snapping sound was gruesome.

The rest of that force got distributed through the *gossak's* body, breaking most of its bones, and probably rupturing a lot of internal organs.

Assuming *gossaks had* internal organs.

Sounds lethal, doesn't it?

Not for a *gossak*.

Part of the reason they were so popular as henchmen. Not only were they tough and vicious, but they could heal from anything short of getting stabbed through the eye with a sprig of holly.

But for now, that *gossak* was well and truly out of the fight.

I grabbed Brikatika myself. Called back over my shoulder.

"How you doing?"

"Bad guys all down." I didn't like how weak Vasco's voice sounded.

"Magellan," I said, "would you come keep an eye on Brikatika while I see to Vasco?"

"No," Vasco said quickly. "We need to get out of here before something comes through those doors."

"Brikatika," I said. "Is anything going to come through those doors?"

"They were going to kill me," Brikatika said, in English. His voice dejected.

"Answer the question or they might not have to."

No, I didn't intend to kill him. But I was more than a little pissed at Brikatika right now, and if he stayed a little edgy, so much the better.

"No," Brikatika said quickly. "Not that I know of. This was supposed to be a safe house. Where I could get a message to—"

"It'll keep," Vasco said, voice weaker still. "We need ... to get out..."

"On it," I said. I started the process of opening a temporary portal to the Upper Forest Park Portal. Nice and out of the way. Someplace we could interview Brikatika in peace.

Only problem was, the portal didn't open.

23

I COULD THINK OF PLACES I WOULDN'T MIND FINDING OUT I WAS trapped. Chief among them, of course, being the bedroom of gorgeous rock star Eva Schmidt.

Assuming, of course, that she wanted me there.

Where I was, though, felt like just about the worst place to discover I was trapped.

A faux-wooden room. Under the Multnomah Channel. Surrounded by wounded and unconscious — and in at least one case, dead — *gossaks*, whose red, furry bodies were still stinking the place up with the odor of wet animal.

Oh, and each wall had a door in it, and any one of those doors might have brought in more enemies at any time. Even though Brikatika insisted this was a safe house, and so even the *gossaks* shouldn't have been here.

Vasco was hurt, and not yet healed. He had some wicked-looking wounds on his chest and arms, from fighting the *gossaks*.

Magellan looked more than a little dinged up himself. Sure he was moving fine, but I didn't like that he'd gotten hurt at all.

There was just something wrong with a creature that would hurt a beagle.

Terrible place to be...

No.

Worse than that.

I was stuck inside a *constructed space* inside a copper veined rock, in the middle of the Multnomah Channel. That meant that this entire place was one big energetic construct, and...

Of course.

I slapped myself in the forehead.

I turned to Vasco, who was gritting his teeth against the pain of applying Bruisebane and Serpent's Kiss to his several injuries.

"Of course I can't just portal us out."

"No," Vasco said as though that were obvious. "You can't portal out of a constructed space. We need to get out of here. But first I..." he growled against the pain and slammed his palm against the floor — "but first I need you to maintain watch until I'm ready for action."

"Isn't there a less painful way to treat our injuries?"

"Yes." Vasco slammed his fist down again while his whole body shook as he continued slathering ointments across this chest wounds. "But nothing ... that works ... this fast."

I checked the doors one at a time, going through their energies to try to find any triggering mechanisms they might have had.

Yes, I was worried about traps even inside a so-called safe house. More than that, though, I was worried about alarms. That maybe, because Brikatika was never supposed to get out of this room alive — speculation on my part, but a decent working theory — if someone passed through the door, either the *dorach* was dead or the *gossaks* had failed.

I didn't find any alerts set up. Any traps either. And I didn't find any kind of hidden doors.

Well. I did find out that two of the doors were fake. But that was less finding a hidden door than finding a hidden section of wall.

I even tried casting my awareness up the three chutes in the ceiling, that were the ways one could enter this room from the outside.

Unfortunately, the design of the place meant that there was no up-the-chutes from here. They were exit-only, and even my awareness could not travel upwards.

While I was doing this checking, Magellan kept Brikatika cornered. Growling the whole time.

Frankly, I think Magellan would have been only too happy to give the big *dorach* a bite for leading us a merry chase. Not to mention getting the poor beagle *gossak*-handled.

He knew better though.

And Brikatika, he just sat there, dejected. His head hanging down.

I itched to ask him questions. But I couldn't do it until Vasco finished his litany of growled swearing, which I would take as a sign that he was healed up and ready to go.

So I did the next best thing.

I checked the unconscious *gossaks* to make sure they weren't going to rouse anytime soon.

As I did that, another Locksmith spell — skill, whatever — occurred to me.

"*Ypnos*," I whispered, with a finger to my lips.

That would keep those unconscious *gossaks* from waking up until we were long gone.

Useful that. Wish it could have worked while they were awake.

Once I was done with them, I gave the room another pass. Didn't find anything more though. But at least, when I finished, Vasco was done.

His green felt shirt was still pretty torn up. Just a sign of how hurt he'd been, in my opinion. He'd seemed to take delight in repairing my own torn clothing when I wasn't looking. But he hadn't found time to fix his own.

That made me give him a closer look.

He was sweaty, and his wild gray hair all matted down. But he looked healthy enough in his tanned, weathered way as he stripped off his shredded shirt.

He didn't bother repairing it. Just stuffed the green felt scraps into his duffel bag, and drew out a red-and-black plaid replacement.

While he buttoned up, I said, "Near as I can tell, the doors aren't trapped."

"Only one is a way out," Vasco said. "The other, if this really was a safe house, will lead to living quarters."

Brikatika pointed to the door to his right.

"Living quarters. Last time I was here, anyway."

"So that's the exit?" I said, pointing to the other door.

"Not how I left last time. There was an exit past the living quarters."

I looked at Vasco. He pulled a spool of red silk cord out of his duffel bag. Even without trying, I could tell that the cord had been worked over, energetically.

I was about to ask a question, but Vasco frowned and shook his head.

He approached Brikatika.

"Paw," Vasco said.

Brikatika extended his left forepaw without looking.

Vasco tied some of the cord around that forepaw. He tied a little more around his own left wrist. He slipped a big combat knife out of his brown hiking boots, then cut the cords from the main spool.

He held the knife up so Brikatika could see it. Or maybe see the energies at play along it. I'm not sure.

Vasco cut the cord that bound them.

"You understand?" Vasco asked the *dorach*.

"I've heard of smithcord," Brikatika said.

The word brought the explanation to my mind. So bound, Brikatika couldn't leave any room Vasco was in. And he couldn't get more than a hundred of Vasco's paces from him, even out in the open.

Vasco tucked the rest of the spool in his duffel, and sheathed his knife.

Next, Vasco used a different paste to treat Magellan's dings and scuffs and likely bruises.

If the ointment caused Magellan any discomfort, I couldn't tell. So I hoped it didn't.

When Vasco finished, he gave the good beagle two treats.

Vasco then stood, drew a deep breath, and popped a restorer in his mouth.

The thought of one of those vitality gumballs made my stomach growl and my muscles complain about how tired they were.

"Need one?" Vasco asked.

"No," I shook my head.

I wasn't nearly as exhausted as I'd normally be after a few good games of basketball, no matter how much my body was trying to tell me otherwise.

"You lead then," Vasco said. "I'll stay rear guard with the prisoner."

I approached the door that might have been an exit. I took the handle in one hand. Assumed a balanced stance and readied my other fist.

"Ready?" I asked.

Magellan yipped. Vasco nodded. Brikatika only stared at the floor.

I ripped the door open.

Another shaft down.

"I don't like the look of this," I said. "Smells like a trap."

"Let me check," Vasco said.

I almost objected. But he *had* been doing this a lot longer than I had. So I let him be the one to send his awareness down the shaft.

It also meant I was right at hand when he started to dive forward.

"Hey!" I grabbed Vasco by the collar and yanked him backwards.

His good flannel shirt started to rip. And Vasco gave me no help. It was as though his mind was already down at the end of the shaft, just waiting for his body to join him.

I grabbed his shoulder with my left hand. Planted one foot on the wall.

Not enough.

I needed both feet on that wall. I needed every ounce of strength I had, and every erg of magic I could bring to bear.

And Vasco was still edging slowly forward.

"Magellan," I said through gritted teeth. "Little help?"

Magellan jumped forward and nipped Vasco's ankle.

Maybe it was the shock of the nip. Maybe it was a signal the two of them had previously established for themselves. Whatever it was, that little bite on the ankle did the trick.

Vasco's mind was back. He shook his head.

But his body was still edging forward against everything I could do to keep him where he was.

I tried to speak, but only managed a strained grunt.

But now Vasco could add his strength to mine. And maybe more important, his own magic.

Vasco planted a hand on each side of the doorway, focused all his renewed strength and energies, and shoved himself backwards.

That did the trick.

We tumbled back onto the supposedly wooden floor, which felt a lot more like stone than wood.

The door slammed shut.

"So," I said through heavy breaths. "I'm thinking that's not the way out."

"There you're wrong," Vasco said, rolling to his feet and offering me a hand up.

"But—"

"That's likely a permanent way out." Vasco turned to Brikatika. "Clearly they want you dead. Can't wait to find out why."

"We should interview him now," I said. "Before something else happens."

"No," Vasco said, voice firm and a dismissive little shake of his head. "We need to get us out of here before reinforcements arrive. Or worse."

He nodded with his head toward that fate he'd narrowly avoided.

"That someone set that up meant they thought Brikatika here might evade his *gossaks*."

"Or *hris* was cleaning house," I said. "Killing the *gossaks* when they tried to leave."

Vasco gave me an approving look. "Not bad. But either way, we need to get out of here before *hris* simply shuts the constructed space down."

Now that ... hadn't occurred to me.

Constructed spaces, from what little I suddenly remembered knowing about them, were neither cheap, nor easy to set up. Collapsing one would mean giving up a valuable resource.

Of course, given that Locksmiths now knew about this one, its value might be plummeting rapidly...

Something rippled through the energies of the constructed space.

"So," I said, "the other door then?"

"And quick," Vasco concurred.

24

I WAS ONLY TOO GLAD TO BE GETTING OUT OF THAT WOODEN ROOM AND the wet-animal smell of unconscious *gossaks*. Especially if this constructed space might collapse any minute.

"Wait," I said, my hand on the doorknob. "What about the *gossaks*? We can't just *leave* them here to get crushed when this place collapses."

"Fine," Vasco said through gritted teeth.

He opened his duffel bag. He also chanted some words I didn't understand, which I thought was quite unfair.

But the words still worked their magic. The *gossaks* all got sucked into Vasco's duffel bag like it was a super-strength vacuum cleaner. If those hulking beasts added an ounce to its weight, Vasco didn't show it.

He just snapped that duffel bag up again, slung it over his shoulder, and impatiently gestured toward the remaining door.

I ripped it open.

That door led into a tight hallway. Fake dark wood all around, with torches in sconces putting out their yellow light and smelling like day-old fireworks.

I took point.

Brikatika galumphed a few steps behind, his otter-like body taking high steps that looked awkward, but had no trouble keeping up. Possibly because...

Vasco followed right on his heels.

Vasco's black-and-red plaid flannel shirt had been fully repaired from the tearing I'd given it trying to keep him from getting sucked down that shaft.

No, I hadn't seen him repair it.

Magellan took rear guard, making sure nothing snuck up on us as we moved down that hall.

And we were moving pretty quickly.

My awareness was stretched out well ahead of me, hunting for traps, enemies, or rooms. And the main thing I kept picking up were little tremors through the energies of the constructed space we moved through.

Tremors that told me this place was going to collapse around us all too soon.

Door ahead on the left...

"Fake." I kept moving.

Another on the right...

"Trapped. Might be the exit past the trap?"

"*No,*" Brikatika said, in *Dorach*. "*Any traps before the living area lead only to holding cells.*"

"Do you know how far to the living area?"

"*The last time I was here, this was all obviously stone. Now it is inobviously stone. I don't know what else has changed.*"

I sighed and kept us moving.

The hallway split in a three-pronged y-shape. I could continue straight ahead, ahead to the right, or ahead to the left.

No. Wait. I couldn't. The left-hand-route didn't exist. It was illusion. I could feel the stone behind the appearance.

But why?

Magellan started barking. No words though.

Just fear.

"It's collapsing," Vasco said. "Pick one and *go.*"

No time to send my awareness down those halls. No time to puzzle through the question with what Brikatika remembered from last time.

I could only rely on my instincts. My own desire to survive.

And my guts were telling me to go right.

I started running down the right-hand passage.

Fake door on the left.

Fake door on the right.

Trapped ceiling door.

"Hug the wall!" I yelled and did so as I passed.

A jet of flame shot down. Brikatika cried out in pain, but a glance said he only got singed. Did we have time to...

Magellan barked from the rear guard. The tunnel behind was collapsing even faster now.

No time then.

I picked up the pace.

Finally. A door ahead of us. No hidden doors on the walls or ceiling or floor. No traps between here and there. Just a final door at the end of the hall.

I didn't trust it for a second. But I didn't have a whole lot of choice.

I hesitated, my hand inches from the doorknob.

Yes, this whole place had been trapped, with an eye toward killing Brikatika. But whoever built it or owned it, *hris* still wanted to use the space *hriself*. No way *hris* wouldn't leave *some* kind of escape hatch.

So there had to be a way out.

But that person wouldn't want to risk Brikatika getting out...

"Running out of hallway back here," Vasco called urgently.

Clarity, thanks to a sudden influx of memory.

Some doors opened to two places.

I started laughing, which got all three of my companions swearing at me.

I didn't have time for them though. Especially not now that I could hear the grind of river stone reasserting itself into the constructed space behind us.

I played my awareness not just along the door itself, but along the doorjamb, the knob, the hinges. I sought a connection that wouldn't be obvious.

"Scott." Vasco sounded worried, but I didn't have time for him.

There.

A tiny filament of green energies, tucked inside a swirl of yellow and blue. A vague sense of low thrum among the crackling of the other tones. The hint of a honey smell inside a stronger fragrance of peanut butter.

That was all the hint I could find of what I was looking for.

It was enough.

I triggered the hidden option in the door. Opened it wide.

And just like that, I was cold, wet, and surrounded by the Mult-nomah Channel.

But I was out of that constructed space.

Brikatika and Vasco came through next, at the same time, and Magellan followed only a moment behind.

All four of us swam for the surface. Came out onto the shore of Sauvie Island.

Dark brown sand and lots of rocks. Scrub grass no more than a dozen feet away, and not much of it between us and the nearest road.

Big, rusty truck rattled past on that road. Sounded like it was slowly murdering its muffler, and it smelled as though it were burning more oil than gas, but neither the truck nor the driver paid us any mind.

The sun was high overhead. Just how long had we been inside that rock?

The rumble of my stomach insisted that we had been in there far too long, and that my Denver omelet breakfast might as well have been eaten during the last ice age.

The warmth of that sun was welcome, though, after the wet cold of the river. Especially with a decent breeze adding a little chill.

Now that I was aware of my temperature tolerance though, I noticed that, after the initial shock, the cold from the Willamette didn't bother me as much as I would have expected.

I was, however, soaking wet again.

I turned to say something. Not sure I recall exactly what. *Possibly* a complaint about being wet. I'd like to think I was more likely to have said something about what we were going to do next.

Whatever I was thinking, I didn't get to say it. Soon as I turned, Vasco had a portal open.

Red as a neon "open" sign, this portal was around its rim. And that same red light sort of ... fluttered in towards its middle, through a field of black. It smelled of good, greasy hamburgers and salty fries, and it sounded like the clattering of dishware.

I didn't even ask where the portal led. I just stepped through, confident it was leading someplace safe, and that Vasco, Brikatika and Magellan would follow.

For once, the sensory cues of a portal suited the destination.

I was standing in a diner.

No. Not just any diner.

I was standing in The Porthole.

I'd never been to The Porthole, of course. But every instructor had raved about it. I recognized it from their descriptions alone.

First, the smell. Rich, dark coffee. Smelled high quality. I mean, I didn't even drink coffee, but this smell had me reconsidering that policy.

I know. It didn't smell like its portal had. But so far as I could tell, no place really did.

Anyway, the floor was tiled in this rainbow swirl pattern that really, should have been obnoxious. But it was done in dim enough shades that it didn't overpower the eye.

The ceiling and walls had the look and texture of lunar rock. Which made perfect sense to me, because this particular diner was inside the moon.

No. I don't know how they made it habitable. But if I had to guess, I'd call it magic and Vasco'd call it "Locksmith skills." Likely skills related to those that were used to create space inside a physical object.

Sure would have helped if my memories had kicked in there, but the related skills felt like they were beyond my training.

Too bad. Wouldn't have sucked to add a room to my apartment.

The Porthole was decorated in a nautical theme. All over the walls were images of boats and sailing. Rigging hung along the ceiling, as well as broken oars long enough to have been used on old Viking vessels.

The tabletops were fashioned from old shipping barrels, but wide enough to seat eight.

And they had seating accommodations to handle any of the species I'd seen, and plenty I hadn't met yet. I knew that, even though I didn't see any of those odd accommodations at the moment.

The chairs I *could* see looked like the kind I'd expect to see on a film set, but with netting instead of cloth for the seat and seatback.

There was also a counter that looked as though it had been cobbled together from old figureheads. And I don't just mean mermaids and monarchs. Squids, sharks, lizardfolk — all manners of figureheads had given their lives to have their tops flattened and lacquered into The Porthole's counter.

Behind the counter right now was a hotheaded little guy named Willy Pete. Wasn't his real name, but then no leprechauns went by their real names.

Willy Pete got his handle because his temper was said to be hot as white phosphorous. Though he claimed it was because his smile was that bright.

Had the kind of blue-black skin that usually suggested African heritage. But Willy Pete was definitely a leprechaun, and stood no taller than my waist. He dressed in black leather and spikes, like he'd walked off the set of an old 80s heavy metal video. Wore his hair in a big cloud of tight red curls.

A sprinkling of Locksmiths were having their lunches, but I had no attention for them. Now that I knew where I was, and that we weren't in immediate danger, I turned back to the entrance.

The Porthole had no front door. Just a permanent portal. Open right now, with its fluttering of red energies, though when it closed I knew it would just look like a smooth, round spot in the lunar wall.

Vasco, Magellan, and Brikatika came through the portal.

The portal closed behind them.

Sure enough, smooth, round lunar wall where the portal had been.

"Grab a table anywhere," Willy Pete called over, his big smile in place. "Geri'll be with you in a moment."

"Can we use the back room?" Vasco called back. "We need some privacy. Oh, and we may have to leave in a hurry."

That wiped the smile off Willy Pete's face. He raised a threatening finger.

"Do *not* make a mess back there."

"Wouldn't dream of it," Vasco assured him, and led Brikatika the right direction, around to the left of the counter, through an unpopulated section of tables.

Magellan's tail was already going a mile-a-minute as he followed, likely anticipating table scraps.

I checked the portal again — still closed — and then fell into rear-guard position.

I knew we needed the information we were about to get from Brikatika. I knew we would probably have to act on it in a hurry.

But I did hope I got to eat first. This place had a great rep. And I was *starving*.

25

THE BACK ROOM AT THE PORTHOLE HAD ONLY ONE TABLE.

A card table.

Not the fancy kind either, like you'd see in a poker room. No, this was a square aluminum job, with a vinyl top, and skinny, fold-out legs that locked into position.

I used to use a table like this one as my kitchen table. Before Katy made me get rid of it. Said mine was too cheap, and she hated the cigarette burn in the vinyl, leftover from my old roommate, Bruce.

The Porthole must have bought this card table the same place I got mine. Even had the same kind of unpadded folding chairs my butt knew so well.

Had to admit though. Table suited the back room, here at The Porthole.

No fancy tiling or fanciful seafaring decorations back here. The floor was rough, gray moonrock. Just like the walls and ceiling. One of the walls had a little slide-up aluminum window shade. Same wall had a cheap, unpainted wooden door, with a tarnished brass handle.

The back room didn't smell like rich coffee either. More like stale cigarettes.

Soon as I closed the big red door behind me, I wanted to rip it back open, for the ventilation. I knew Vasco would never go for it though.

Privacy was the point. Not comfort.

Speaking of privacy...

I looked the room over one more time. Just the one other entrance or exit, apart from possible portals.

Not exactly the kind of back room I'd expect in a restaurant, either. I mean, no way this was set up for private parties.

Had to be a break room, didn't it? What were the odds that a restaurant would keep an interrogation room?

Vasco went right up to what I'd thought was a window shade. Opened it, and I could hear now that it went straight into the kitchen.

Sounded like a dozen workers back there, prepping and cooking.

Vasco reached inside and slid out an aluminum shelf that locked into place as though it were part of the windowsill.

"Cup of black coffee, please," Vasco called inside. "And a bowl of Magellan's favorite, if you would."

He turned to Brikatika, who was frowning at the accommodations.

"Want anything?" Vasco asked the *dorach*.

"A *dorach* seat would be nice."

"Not in the back room." Sounded like a woman's voice. The kind of voice that suggested this woman had been waiting tables since the Industrial Revolution, and had been chain-smoking the entire time. "Can pass you a mat."

"Fine," Brikatika said, and started pulling a chair back, using his teeth.

The mat came through first. Blue. Looked like something I'd expect to see kids lying on in a pool. Vasco handed it to me, and I brought it to Brikatika, who twitched his whiskers in disdain, but unrolled it and sat down on it.

"Get some food," Vasco said to me, then called through the window. "All of this on my tab, all right?"

"All right," the voice called back. Honestly, this woman's voice sounded as though speaking hurt her.

I tried to smile as I stepped up to the window. Inside there were only about a half-dozen people working, but fast and efficient.

Four of the workers were *vomvos*, humanoid bees. More or less. I mean, they stood like humans, and their buzzing could mimic any number of languages.

But they had wings on their backs, and six thin, black limbs. Two of the limbs were used like legs, and the other four were all busy, either dealing with dishware, washing, or food prep.

I think I considered *vomvos* humanoid because all six of their limbs ended in appendages like fingers and thumbs. They were naked, though, except for their aprons and white hats.

The other two people back there were humans. One, an old Asian woman in a white chef's outfit. Which meant she was probably Profundia, the famous cook who was said to be able to make any dish from any world, and make it better than the natives.

The other person was a woman in a rainbow-colored waitress uniform. Younger than I expected. Maybe about my age. She had dark caramel skin, long, black hair, and sleek, lupine good looks. Geri, I presumed.

"Please," I said, not sure whom I should be addressing, "I'd like a burger, medium rare, with swiss cheese. Side of curly fries. And a Diet Eruption Cola, easy on the ice."

Nobody responded.

"Um, thank you," I said, and turned away.

Vasco was already seated on one chair. Magellan perched on another, his paws up on the folding table and head high enough that he could see. Brikatika sat on his mat in the place of the third seat, leaving the last for me.

"Coffee up, and a bowl of mixed chicken."

The voice that said those words sounded as nondescript as any Midwest newscaster.

The chime of a bell followed the words. By the time I turned around, no one was standing there.

I grabbed the bowl and coffee cup, and brought them over to the table. Magellan started eating happily. Vasco didn't even look at his coffee.

"Who were you trying to contact?" Vasco asked Brikatika, as I sat.

"Look," Brikatika said. "What you need to understand is that I'm out. I'm not involved anymore. I thought they were willing to let me go, but—"

"Hey, hey, hey," I said, assuming the role of the good cop. Wasn't something covered in Locksmith training, but hey, I'd seen my share of movies and TV shows. "You know I don't want to see anything bad happen to you. I've saved your life twice already. But—"

"Is he serious?" Brikatika said to Vasco, pointing one paw at me.

"This isn't game time," Vasco said, grimacing at me. He turned back to Brikatika. "You know how bad this can go for you. We need to know who you were trying to contact, and we need to know who 'they' are."

"I need assurances," Brikatika said. "The clock is running on this."

"Why?" I asked. "What do you mean the clock is running?"

"Yeah," Vasco said. "You could have mentioned that before."

"Burger up," said that disturbingly nondescript voice that *had* to be one of the *vomvos*. "Medium rare, with a side of curly fries and Diet Eruption Cola."

I ran to grab my food while Brikatika and Vasco argued briefly.

I tossed a couple of fries into my mouth on my way back to the table.

They were so good I had to catch myself from stumbling.

Fries were one of those fast food stables that were just ... filler. They could be crispy and good, or they could be spicy and good, but even at their best I knew they were just a way of using potatoes to fill my belly.

The curly fries at The Porthole were something more than that.

They were light. So light I could probably have stuffed them into my mouth all day without stopping and not been the least bit sorry.

They were the perfect blend of crispy outside and textured inside, so that their initial taste popped, but then their secondary taste filled my mouth.

And that taste. A blend of spices I couldn't quite parse, though I could taste garlic, basil and paprika all blending together well around some kind of marvelous base.

I missed the next few things Vasco and Brikatika said as I sat and popped more fries into my mouth.

"Burger!" Magellan barked at me. "Taste better with the burger."

Vasco whistled, sharp and sudden. Brought my focus, and Magellan's, from the food and back to the conversation.

"Sorry," I said.

"No," Vasco said. "Forgot this was your first visit. I shouldn't have brought you here for the first time when I need your attention. Drink your soda. Save some of those fries for later." He raised his voice. "Need a to-go box for that burger."

Turned his attention back to Brikatika.

"No more bullshit. You need to lay it all out now or—"

"If you banish my family from earth, they'll find us. There's nowhere for us to run now."

"Look," I said, trying to keep from looking longingly back at my plate, while my stomach rumbled forlornly. "Obviously you violated the Va-a-naska Treaty, or you wouldn't be working so hard for a deal. Helping us now will work in your favor, but we still have to consider what you've done."

"So your best hope," Vasco said, "is helping us stop the people you're worried about."

"That means," I said, picking up the thread, "the sooner you give us everything, the more we can do to help you."

"Make us wait too long," Vasco continued as though we'd rehearsed this, "and you'll miss your window. Because if we don't stop whatever's coming, you're an accessory."

"I'd say accomplice." I frowned at Vasco.

"That's Janna's call."

"Still," I said, "he's holding back knowledge of treaty violations, and—"

"All right," Brikatika said, shaking his head slowly. "All right."

A ripple of exhaustion ran down his fur.

"There are more rocks like the one I took you guys to. A half-dozen I know of, but there might be more. The ones I know are scattered along the Willamette and Columbia Rivers. Using the Portland area as a testing ground."

"Smuggling?" Vasco said.

Brikatika nodded.

"*Gossaks* bring the contraband through at a murder site. Hand it off to *nychtera* who get the contraband overland to a holding rock by the river. I would pick it up at the river and bring it downtown to the distribution site."

Nychtera. Those were the large bats I saw during my first trip to Locksmith Central — aka the great prismatic cavern.

Did that mean Chiron was...

Brikatika sat back and waved his paws. "But I'm out. I swear."

"Why?" I asked.

"My oldest just — how would you say it? — formal mating... Got married."

Of course. Generations were a factor in the Va-a-naska Treaty. Banishment was a common form of punishment, for any treaty violations, and could be extended to immediate family, but not extended family.

Once Brikatika's oldest child got married, then *hris* would become extended family, as defined in the Va-a-naska Treaty. If Brikatika got banished, his wife and unmarried children might be banished with him — depending on the violation — but any married progeny and their offspring?

He might never see or hear from them again.

"Who were you running to?" Vasco said.

"Quelan," Brikatika said, shaking his head. "She made the holding zones. But she told me she didn't trust the Network. Told me she'd help me if I needed to get out. Told me—"

"Quelan lies," Vasco said, his voice as gentle as I'd ever heard it. "I'd like to say Quelan only follows the money, but she's never that simple. Still. The only thing you can rely on about Quelan, is that you can't rely on her."

Brikatika nodded, whiskers sad and sagging.

"What about your family?" Vasco asked.

"Mated *doracha* can always find each other. She would have followed this evening, once I'd established it was safe."

"Is Quelan behind the Network?" I asked, getting us back to the topic at hand.

"No," Brikatika and Vasco said at the same time.

Brikatika's whiskers shivered in surprise, but Vasco said, 'Not her style. I don't doubt she contracted for the holding rocks, and at least one so-called safe house. But gigs she runs herself are simpler than that Network sounds. Simpler and more dangerous. She might be using the Network to test something for herself though."

"So who is behind the Network then?" I asked. "Chi—"

I never got to finish that question though.

The red door burst open.

A bluebird flew into the room.

Janna's voice came out of the bluebird, as it approached the card table.

"Brikatika's family is reported missing."

"No!" Brikatika moaned. "They wouldn't!"

The bluebird faded away as soon as its message was heard.

"We have to go," Vasco said to me. "Pack your burger."

"Take me with you," Brikatika said.

"Forget it," Vasco said, coming to his feet. "They already want to kill you. I'll grab one of the other 'Smiths to get you to Janna for a full debriefing while Scott and I go after your family."

"This is a trap," I said, standing now myself. "Has to be. They'll know we—"

"You *need* me," Brikatika said. "I can find my mate faster than you ever could."

Vasco sighed, but he knew the *dorach* was right.

"Fine," Vasco said, then turned to me. "Hurry up with that burger. We need to move."

26

Now, Locksmiths can't just open up a portal to anywhere they want to go. No matter how much it may seem like it sometimes.

Fact is, there are two major ways a Locksmith can travel by portal.

The easiest and most certain is to use a permanent portal as an anchor. That gives us a big advantage over most people who want to use a portal. Most people have to be on one side of a permanent portal, and open it directly to the other side.

Locksmiths, though, can open a portal from anywhere, more or less, linking it temporarily with any permanent portal they know.

The second way, which is more than a little bit trickier, is to fashion a portal that's temporary on both ends. In other words, *without* the benefit of a permanent portal as anchor.

Takes more skill and effort to work that way, but a temporary portal could, in theory, lead from anywhere to anywhere.

In practice, though, it leads from wherever the Locksmith is standing to someplace the Locksmith is capable of going.

It's that last part that's the real trick.

Ultimately, what it means, is that as a Locksmith, I could open a temporary portal to anywhere I could see, or that I knew well enough to have a good sense of the place.

Going to my parents' house? Where I grew up? That would be a piece of cake. Especially if I used doorways on both ends.

Natural transition points are easier to work with than just ripping out a portal in mid-air.

Anyway, going to my current apartment? Same thing. Easy-peasy.

Going to Riverfront Park by the basketball courts? *Pretty* safe jump. Having been there once for a decent period of time, odds were pretty good that I could get there.

Of course, I hadn't been there since I'd been *trained*, which meant that my *sense* of Riverfront Park might not have been as good as I wanted it to be.

The training, after all, had taught me to feel the flow of time, and refined my sense of space in ways I couldn't have dreamed of, before.

I likely wouldn't chance opening a portal to Riverfront Park, without the opportunity to visit again first.

Making a mistake with a temporary portal could lead to ... unexpected destinations. Worlds that are *very much* like the intended target...

But *wrong*. Sometimes in very dangerous ways.

So there was no way Vasco or I could have portaled the four of us (including Brikatika and Magellan, of course) directly to Brikatika's mate. Even if Brikatika were somehow able to describe where she was.

Instead, we had to come close, and do our best.

So as soon as my magnificent, uneaten burger was packed safely in its to-go box and stored in Vasco's seemingly endless duffel bag, I used the red doorway to open a portal to someplace close to the river, and that I was certain I could get us to.

The Ross Island Portal.

Thus, once more I opened the way back to that ugly, dirty sliver of rock in the Willamette River, known by the wrong name: Toe Island.

I was, however, paranoid enough to check the portal first, to make sure no one had managed to trap it.

The portal was clean.

I stepped through...

Bad idea.

Turned out that the portal might not have been trapped, but the rocky surface on the other side of that portal *was*.

I found myself stuck, knee deep in the rocks of Toe Island. Worse, I couldn't feel any energies right now. Any of them. Not the flow of time or space, or even any of the magic that I knew was around me.

I couldn't feel the energies of the open portal in the rock behind me.

I couldn't feel the energies of the trap.

I couldn't feel the energies flowing through my own *body*, which I would normally have tapped for a spell/skill to try to free myself.

I couldn't even feel the presence of the earth spirits that were usually hanging around the portal.

All I could feel was a sense of cold numbness, spreading from my feet on up as I sank into the rocks. Exhausting cold. Every muscle touched by it started cramping until it went numb.

Nothing I could reach to pull myself out.

A pair of jet skis rocketed past, going north. I tried to call out to them, but I couldn't open my mouth to speak.

My frantic waving was ignored, of course.

Everyone knew nobody actually went to Toe Island. Work into that the magics of the trap, and I could die here in front of all of Portland, and every single person would be likely to turn away as I did.

I tried to close off the portal, but I couldn't even do that.

The cold had spread up into my thighs now, but that was where I stopped sinking. Which was a small blessing, at least.

Very small, as it turned out.

I could see the flicking tail of an alligator approaching.

There weren't supposed to be alligators in the Willamette, of course. Especially not alligators that had to measure six feet across, and I couldn't even guess how long.

That is to say, an alligator big enough to eat me in a single swallow.

I was the point man. If this side was trapped, I was supposed to slam closed the portal to save the others. Give Vasco a chance to evade the trap and come through at his nearest known location. Maybe even get here in time to save my life.

Little chance of that.

I couldn't close the portal. I couldn't send a warning. And that gator was seconds away from opening those jaws.

I did the only thing I could think of.

I ripped off my good, wet silk shirt, buttons flying, and threw it back through the portal before Vasco and the others could come through.

I turned back to meet my fate.

"Come on," I taunted, psyching myself up. I had adrenaline flowing now. At least, from the waist up. I might not have had Locksmith skills to rely on, but the training had included plenty of physical work.

Those jaws snapped open wide. Hot breath overpowered the merely warm breeze. Breath that stank of raw meat and blood.

I tucked in my arms. Fists clenched.

"Come on," I said again, more to myself than anything else. "Come on, you big ugly beastie."

The jaws snapped together. Lower jaw in front of my waist and upper jaw somewhere behind my head.

I slammed out my fists against those collapsing jaws with every ounce of strength in my body.

Got my fists inside the teeth. Felt like I was caught in a hot, wriggling meat vise.

My whole body shook with effort.

Little bits inside me popped and cracked and complained.

But I held those jaws apart.

Didn't have long, though. Its jaws were made to do what it was doing. My limbs weren't.

I roared. Pain from the strain. My need to live. All these things I poured into keeping those jaws apart.

But those teeth started getting closer.

Suddenly the giant alligator rocketed backwards.

Its jaws clamped shut as it went, raking grooves in my arms.

But missing the rest of me.

I looked up to see...

I started laughing as much from disbelief as anything else.

I looked up to see Magellan. Giant sized, against the rich blue afternoon sky. Easily sixty feet tall at the shoulder. His hind paws were on Ross Island proper. His forepaws were in the Willamette.

And his jaws had clamped down on the tail of the "giant" alligator.

Magellan worried it like a bone, then flung it way north. We were a few miles from where the Willamette met the Columbia, and I was pretty sure that alligator was Washington bound.

I just kept laughing. Overjoyed to be alive. Amazed at the sight I'd just seen.

Then Magellan was normal sized again, and standing on the rocks ahead of me, just outside the trap zone, as though he could sniff it.

"I'm the best, aren't I?" Magellan barked happily, jumping and trotting back and forth. "I'm the best beagle in the whole wide world! And *nobody* messes with *my* friends! I should get *so many treats!*"

"Yes, you should," I agreed, laughing. "Soon as I can figure out how to get out of this."

"You can't." Vasco's voice, coming from behind me. "Give me a se... Ah! There it is."

The ground spat me out as my sense of the flow of energies, space and time all flooded back into me.

I landed smoother than I expected, given that life was only just flowing back through my legs.

So much pain. Not just where those gator teeth had ripped the flesh of my arms, either. I really had popped little things inside my shoulders and arms and chest.

And every one of those popped ligaments and tendons started screaming at me.

I still managed to catch my shirt, when Vasco threw it back to me. Entirely dry and repaired, of course.

Not that I could put it on yet. Couldn't stretch my arms that wide yet.

Instead I slung the shirt over my shoulder and dug the jar of Serpent's Kiss and Bruisebane out of my pocket.

All of my muscles clenching in dismayed anticipation at the thought of the pain that lay between me and healed arms.

"Good move, throwing your shirt back through the portal," Vasco said to me as he tossed Magellan treats. "Brikatika and I almost came through. Got your warning just in time."

"Where'd you come through?"

"I know a good spot on Ross Island proper. You should study the land around all the major portals, in case you're the one doing the rescuing next time."

"*We should go,*" Brikatika said in *dorach*, pacing back and forth. Then he shook himself, a ripple of chagrin running down his fur.

"I'm sorry," he said to me in English. "I really am glad you're fine, but—"

"He's not," Vasco said, looking at the blood on my arms. "We need to give him a minute to heal up."

Brikatika whirled on Vasco.

"But I can feel Rakata getting farther away!"

"Good," Vasco said, putting away his treats against the whining protest of Magellan. "That means you have a strong sense of her, and we should be able to follow the trail."

"But—"

"We're not proceeding until Scott's ready."

I gritted my teeth and opened the jar.

I'll leave it at this.

Serpent's Kiss gets more ... unpleasant, the deeper the cuts it's fixing. And the runnels in my arms were *deep*.

As for the Bruisebane, its healing properties did extend to the kind of tendon and ligament damage I'd sustained. But that pain was worse than the Serpent's Kiss.

I was so shaky and soaked through with sweat when I finished healing my arms that I almost didn't want to put my poor, much abused silk shirt back on.

But I couldn't run around without a shirt on. That might actually have *drawn* attention, instead of shunting it away.

Vasco also stuffed a handful of my fries into my mouth, which went a long way toward making me feel human again.

Or at the very least, those spicy curly fries tasted so good they distracted me from the ordeal I'd just endured.

Brikatika didn't wait for us. Dove straight into the Willamette and started swimming.

Didn't do him much good though. With the smithcord around his wrist, he couldn't get far from Vasco.

So Brikatika was forced to wait while Vasco and I prepped for more swimming, then boosted our speed. Vasco boosted Brikatika's speed as well, since no matter how much faster the *dorach* might have become, the smithcord would keep him close by.

Then the four of us dove into the waters of the Willamette, got down near the bottom of the river, and began swimming south at tremendous speeds.

27

BRIKATIKA IN THE LEAD, THE FOUR OF US SWAM AT BREAKNECK SPEEDS down the Willamette River. We stuck to the bottom, of course, where we had to maneuver around rocks, fish, and the occasional confused lizardfolk, but we didn't have to worry about hitting ships or human swimmers.

With the speed boost keeping us from kicking up silt and mud, there wasn't even a cloud of muck to mark our passage. Even if an everyday citizen *wanted* to look down under the water, they wouldn't have spotted anything worth ignoring.

I kept my focus solidly on swimming, taking up the rear. Following Brikatika. Keeping track of Vasco and Magellan. Yet even so, I couldn't help but wonder if Brikatika's experience of the speed boost was the same as mine.

Did the water feel like responsive gelatin to him too? If so, what was that like for his otter-like body?

No way I could ask though, so I tried to busy that portion of my mind with tracking our movement. I hadn't done that the last time I'd been swimming this fast, and the result had been too disorienting for me.

So I knew when we passed out of Portland to the southeast. I knew when we passed by Milwaukie, then Oak Grove. The river bent southwest then, past West Linn, then Oregon City.

All the while we jetted through the water. We didn't even need to surface for air, thanks to the underwater freedom spells.

It was finally southwest of Oregon City that Brikatika slowed enough to point out our target.

It was that tugboat. The little rusty one I'd seen earlier. The one I remembered as smelling like a tire fire. With two passengers in full yellow slickers, hoods up, despite the heat of the day, and the lack of rain.

I resisted the urge to smack Vasco on the shoulder.

I *knew* there was something suspicious about that tugboat.

No other water traffic around us right now, of course. Not with something odd about the tugboat. Chances were pretty good that other boats and such were keeping their distance, without even realizing they were doing it.

Wait.

I was getting used to the idea of normal people ignoring the, well, *abnormal*. Still. There shouldn't have been *enough* odd about that boat for everyday people to ignore it in droves.

The passengers in slickers maybe, but they were strange enough for eyes to slip off them, not strange enough to keep the area clear like this...

I grabbed Vasco by the sleeve. He gave me a puzzled look, which looked even weirder under the water, where his wild gray hair drifted out in all directions.

I shook my head. Pointed to the shore.

Vasco frowned, but he couldn't speak to me any more than I could to him. Not underwater.

We swam for the shore. Magellan fell right into place beside us. Poor Brikatika got dragged along by the smithcord, despite his own efforts to go straight aboard the ship.

We didn't leave the water. None of us. Just bobbed over the surface at the shore, concealed from the tugboat by a jutting rock. This was also a spot where the river bottom was still low enough to keep our bodies submerged, along with the gills on our necks, while our heads came up enough for speech.

Quiet speech. No way of knowing what resources that tugboat and its people could bring to bear.

"Area's clear," I said, as soon as Vasco's and my heads were above water.

"So?" Brikatika said quickly, before even Vasco could reply. "Why aren't we on that boat *right now*?"

Vasco took my hint though. Held up a warning finger to Brikatika, whose whiskers vibrated with irritation.

Vasco and I both turned to extend awareness across the waters to the boat, while Magellan kept a fixed eye on Brikatika.

Sure enough, the energies flitting around that thing included multiple spells. The most obvious of which, to me, was the *don't look here* effect.

"Right," Vasco muttered. "Good catch, rook."

Once we could get our minds past that effect, the wardings became apparent.

Biggest was a detector, that would tell someone in the cabin when anyone boarded the ship, and who it was.

Apart from that, there were a few simple effects. Turned out the rust wasn't real. Just illusion. There were a couple of other illusions as well, making the tugboat look shabbier and messier than it really was.

Even that tire fire smell was an illusion, to help encourage people to spend their attention elsewhere.

"I don't see any traps," I said.

"Tough to be sure from here," Vasco said. "I count the detector as the most obvious trap though. They just detect Locksmiths boarding, and take steps that might not be bound into any energies right this second. They might have someone standing by with the equivalent of a grenade."

"But we *must* board the boat," Brikatika said. "I'll go myself if you're scared."

"We're not scared," Vasco said, though I knew *my* nerves were jangling pretty hard. "But if we do this wrong, they might kill your family rather than risk losing them to a rescue. And none of us want that."

Now, I can't be sure what all had been going through poor Brikatika's mind up to that point. Probably nothing more than just getting to his wife and children as fast as possible. That was what would make the most sense to me, but I was a human.

I could speak *dorach* fluently. But that didn't make me an expert in *dorach* psychology.

Once Vasco pointed out the potential consequences of us pulling a rescue attempt, though, the *dorach's* whiskers dipped in fear, taking his whole head down in a dunk under the water and back up, dripping.

"That is where she is," Brikatika said, pointing with one paw toward the tugboat. "I know that as I know the waters around us, or the air I breathe. But I will stop rushing. I trust you to lead."

"We need to take down that detector," I said. "Know any quick ways?"

"Nope." Vasco shook his head. "One advantage though. We have two of us. You take down the detector. I'll watch everything else. Keep any traps keyed to it from springing, or extra alerts from going off."

Said something about the tenseness of the situation that neither Vasco nor I chuckled at his use of "keyed."

"Can you do that?" Brikatika asked, sounding astonished.

"Not if I have to disable it myself. But if he handles that part, I can make sure the rest is safe."

"Let's go," I said.

Back under the water we went. One advantage of only having stuck our heads out of the water was that our underwater freedom spells were still in effect.

The speed boosts were down, but with the underwater freedom still in effect, we didn't need anything more to keep up with something as slow as that tug.

We swam over as close as we dared, and I went to work on the detectors while Vasco acted as magical overwatch.

Tricky, keeping my awareness on the other side of a *don't notice me* effect long enough to work with the energies. Would have been all too easy to get sloppy. Make a mistake.

So despite my own nervous urgency, I worked slow and sure.

First, I cast my awareness along the whole area around that boat, narrowing it slowly, slowly, slowly, until I was sure I hadn't missed any threads that tied in to someplace else.

The last thing I needed to do was keep the boat from knowing what was going on, but accidentally call in their reinforcements.

Once I established the limits of the detection effect, I allowed myself to perceive it in full detail.

Its color was a pale, watery blue. Its scent was foul. Reminded me of a BART station bathroom I'd been in once, as a teen, on my way back from an A's game.

That was one *nasty* bathroom. And the energies of this alarm effect, they smelled even worse.

Tactilely, the alarm felt like a low electrical pulse. One that was absent, absent, present. That was part of the reason it was tough to spot. It could be looked for three or four times in a row, but if it wasn't pulsing, it might not get noticed.

Once I had a true sense of the detection effect, then I only needed to find its keystone.

This time the "keystone" reference made me smile.

"Key" is a joke word to a Locksmith for good reason. Not only could we lock and unlock portals — when it came to locking and unlocking things, controlling admittance, we were the best at it.

Truly. The best.

Not a boast, either. Of all the various races that ever came our way or interacted with us in any ways, none were as good as Locksmiths when it came to gaining access and controlling access.

Locks and keys were tied into the philosophies behind our skills and magics. For example, the underwater freedom effect was done through "unlocking" water, in a deeper sense.

So while a *listasa* elf might unweave a spell, or a *sissalaxa* lizardfolk might eat the heart of its power, I could disable an effect by unlocking it.

In the case of that magical alarm, the point that held it together — the lock — lay between the two absent pulses of the cycle, in the heart of a urinal odor, where the watery blue edged closer to a color-less white.

That was my target. Time to pick the lock.

Diakopi. I could only think the incantation, but that was enough to combine with a poking gesture to unravel that detection effect and open the boat to us.

Vasco made the same gesture, a fraction of a second behind mine. I wasn't sure exactly what he'd done, but he gave me a thumb's up.

I swam down to the riverbed, then back up as fast as I could.

I sprang up into the air, water sheeting out around me, and grabbed onto a hot, dusty tire on the side of the boat.

The underwater freedom effect broke as soon as I was out of the water, and I was bone dry again.

I scrambled up the tires, rolled over the gunwale, and crouched down on the rough wooden deck of the tugboat.

No one visible from...

Check that. No one visible *on the deck.* Inside the cabin, I could see the skinny, bearded man from earlier at the wheel. His gaze was fixed and distant.

I could detect a haze of foreign energies flowing around his head. I doubted he was in control of his own actions. Likely another treaty violation...

The rest of the deck looked clear.

That worried me more than a little. There was only the one cabin on this little tugboat, and it didn't look big enough to...

Check that. Now that I was inside the illusions surrounding the boat, I could tell that the cabin had several energetic effects flowing around it.

At a glance, none of them looked dangerous or deceptive, so I finished my job.

I stuck my arm out over the water and waved.

Brikatika was out of the water, up the tires, and beside me before I even pulled my arm back.

I hushed him, and he nodded, slow and awkward as the gesture looked on his otter-like body.

Vasco came up — slower than Brikatika — a moment later. Magellan under one arm, and his duffel bag still slung over his shoulder.

Magellan was handed over the rail first. Good boy that he was, he knew to get low and stay quiet without my telling him.

The duffel bag came next, and as I grabbed it and set it down, I vowed that whatever container I chose to carry with me — once I'd had time to make it bottomless, like the duffel bag — would be smaller than a freaking *duffel bag*.

Vasco came last. Dry as the rest of us. His eyes raked across the boat, and I could tell he'd drawn the same conclusions I had.

Staying low, I led the way across the deck to the entrance to the cabin.

It should have looked like a red doorway.

Instead it looked like a gray, stone tunnel entrance, leading straight into blackness.

"*Nychter* magic," Vasco whispered. "They make their own caves so they don't interfere with the normal bats of worlds they travel to."

"That's real?" I couldn't keep the shock out of my whispered words.

Vasco nodded. "No further wards, either."

"Come into my parlor," I muttered, shaking my head.

Vasco thumped me lightly on the shoulder. Gave me a wicked smile.

"Remember, Scott. *We're* the spiders here."

I nodded grimly, and turned to the tunnel.

28

BEFORE SETTING FOOT INTO THE DARKNESS OF THE TUNNEL, I PRESSED my palms to my eyes and whispered the incantation, *"Fos."*

I could now see the tunnel ahead of me, as though it were just on the bright edge of twilight.

The tunnel was narrow. Narrow enough that I couldn't have put my arms out to the sides, if I needed to. Once past the opening, though, the ceiling went up quickly to at least three times my height.

The ground under my feet was rocky and dirty and gray.

The air of the tunnel smelled of dust and ... bats.

At least, I was pretty sure that smell was bats. I didn't know what about them generated it, but I'd visited the bat exhibits in a number of zoos over the years, and this tunnel's scent reminded me of all of them.

And between that dry, musky odor and the all-too-recent public toilet smell I'd had to endure, my rumbling stomach was happy I hadn't gotten to eat yet. I didn't have anything to bring back up, if the odors got any worse.

I stretched my awareness out ahead of me, as much to make sure that there weren't any traps waiting as because...

There.

Maybe three, four paces in. Weak spot in the floor would open into a pit.

Without opening it, I couldn't be positive, but I was *pretty* sure it was a pit, down there, not a shaft.

So I crept up just shy of it, and waved the others to approach.

"No deeper tricks to it," Vasco whispered when he reached me. "You want to lock it or shall I?"

"What if it's the way down that they use?"

"*Nychters* are a lot like bats," Vasco said, patiently. "Would a bat use that? Or would it go up?"

I ducked my head, a little sheepish.

The design might have been a pit trap, but really, it was just a concealed trap door, above a stone chamber.

I reached down to just above the stones of the pit trap.

"*Konta*," I whispered, while making a twisting, locking gesture.

I then strolled across the pit trap, followed by Magellan, Brikatika, and Vasco.

Once across, Vasco turned and reached to unlock the pit trap. Standard procedure to not leave signs of our passage.

I still grabbed him by the shoulder.

"What if we have to leave in a hurry?" I whispered.

Vasco frowned, but nodded, and left the pit trap locked.

There were three more traps like that one, irregularly spaced farther down the tunnel. The first two we handled the same way.

The last of those three pit traps, though, was the worst.

Somebody had already triggered this one. Or maybe it just never had any stone covering at all.

Either way, there was nothing to lock. It was just an open pit.

It filled the the tunnel from side to side, and was long enough that I couldn't just step over it. I might not have been able to jump over it either. Felt to me like just over thirty-five feet long.

What was worse, the tunnel had widened to about ten feet across by this point. So I couldn't even walk myself across like a rock climber, using my hands on one rock wall and my feet on the other.

Jumping looked like the only answer. But that was a problem.

Not for me, necessarily. I mean, I could jump well, from all that basketball, even before my Locksmith training. After training, a thirty-foot jump might just have been possible.

But just because *I* might make it across, didn't mean Vasco would. And even if he did, Brikatika wouldn't.

Magellan, well, I wouldn't have thought Magellan could do it. Then again, I wouldn't have thought the beagle could grow to sixty feet at the shoulder, but I'd seen it with my own eyes.

So I couldn't really discount anything, as far as Magellan went.

"Energy net?" I asked in hushed tones. "Cover the top and cross that way?"

"Too much energy," Vasco said. "Someone would notice. Give up our surprise."

Instead Vasco dug into his duffel bag. Came out with a rope cargo net, a hammer, and a couple of spikes.

"*That* won't draw attention?" I asked.

"Won't warn them that we're Locksmiths."

Vasco tacked the cargo net into the rocks about a foot above the floor, on both sides of the tunnel.

He handed me the other two spikes and the hammer, then made an *after you* gesture.

I sighed. Backed up a few steps. Bounced up and down a couple of times to get my legs ready. That was habit, though. All that swimming had my legs as ready to go as they might need to be.

If anything was likely to be a problem, it was that I hadn't had any protein since that Denver omelet, oh so many hours ago now.

I ran right up to the edge of that pit.

I leapt for all I was worth.

I came up short.

Soon as I realized I was bound for the pit wall, I pulled in my arms and legs. Braced for impact.

I slammed into the far side of the pit. Air *whuffed* out of me.

I bounced off the wall. Started falling. Flailed with my hands for something to grab.

One hand caught part of the rope cargo net. Vasco had to have thrown it.

I didn't question. I grabbed it. Clung for dear life while my pulse tried to beat its way right out of my throat.

Sure enough, Vasco was holding the other side, in case the anchors gave out under my falling weight.

The cargo net and I slammed into the side of the pit wall.

Less momentum this time, but the collision still hurt.

I could see now that the pit walls had squared edges. And that the shaft into the pit went on for a good hundred feet or so. I could see bones down at the bottom as well.

Human bones.

Well, the remains of human bones, anyway. They weren't exactly intact skeletons. That status of those skeletons, though, wasn't what mattered to me at the moment.

More important just then? Apart from getting my ass out of this trap?

The fact that treaty violations just kept stacking up today.

I gripped the net. Calmed myself down, against the pounding of my heart and the clutching of my sphincter. Not to mention my most recent set of aches and bruises.

I started climbing the rope net back up to the ledge.

"All right," Vasco said, pulling me up onto his side of the pit, where I lay for a moment and reassured myself that I had not, in fact, fallen to my death.

"All right," Vasco said again, reassuringly this time. "Think you're up to another attempt?"

"I didn't make it last time. Why should this one work?"

"Because this time you'll be ready." He clapped me on the shoulder. "You were only about a foot shy. If you'd been ready, you could have grabbed the other side with your hands and pulled yourself up."

I didn't feel very certain of that.

"I'd really rather open a portal to the other side."

"No," Vasco said, shaking his head firmly. "Right now, the *nychtera* probably know *someone* is in their tunnels. You made more than a little noise slamming into rock walls. They'll send a couple of scouts to check."

Vasco gave me a grim smile. "But if you open a portal they'll *know* Locksmiths are in the tunnel. They'll hit us in force before we can be ready."

"Who else could end up in these tunnels?"

"Whose bones were those at the bottom of the pit?"

I sighed, but couldn't find fault with his logic.

I stood. Rolled my shoulders. Took a few deep breaths (that were too dusty for my taste). Did a couple of deep knee bends.

"You're vacillating," Vasco whispered.

"Fine," I grumbled.

I bounced a couple of times. Set myself. And ran for all I was worth.

I leapt, right at the edge.

Tried to fling myself even farther, once I was in the air, not that it would do much good.

I started coming down.

I wasn't going to make it.

My teeth gritted. My heart double-timed it. I tried not to think about the sweat in my eyes, or worse, the sweat no doubt on my hands.

I landed chest-first against the edge of the pit. Sharp ache through my ribs. My lungs seized up. Couldn't breathe.

But I could grip. I grasped the rocky floor of the other side of the pit trap with everything I had. My fingers had to double-time it against the sweat on my palms.

I yanked myself up and over. Rolled over onto my back and tried to persuade my lungs to breathe again.

Before I finished, the edge of the rope cargo net hit me in the face.

I grabbed it by reflex. Held it tight while my lungs and diaphragm remembered how to inhale and exhale.

Once life-giving air was coming into me once again, I rolled to my knees and tacked the cargo net to the rocks on this side of the pit trap.

Then I just lay back and waited while Vasco, Brikatika and Magellan made their way across.

While I waited, I tried not to think about the rustling sounds I heard further down the tunnel, around where it snaked to the right before cutting back left again.

Once the others joined me, it was our turn to lay a little trap. Vasco and I worked together to weave an energy net like a spider's web across the tunnel behind us.

Only took a moment, and it reminded me of what Vasco'd said only a few minutes before. *We're the spiders*. Climbing nets. Weaving traps. We really were like spiders down in this tunnel.

Soon as our trap was in place, the four of us got prone against the floor and walls. Tried to make ourselves less noticeable to sonar.

A pair of *nychtera* flew around the bend toward us, at speed.

They zoomed right into our energy net. Caught there like flies. Unable to even screech out a warning.

Their yellow eyes bored into us as they wished their teeth could. And those teeth were big enough to do some serious harm.

I hadn't gotten a sense of how big those *nychtera* were, back in the prismatic crystal chamber. I'd seen them either at long-distances, or with only Chiron nearby for scale.

I'd known the *nychtera* looked like big yellow bats. I hadn't realized they were the size of great danes.

And there were how *many* of these things ahead of us?

"Maybe we should call in backup?" I asked, trying to suppress the hope in my voice.

"No time," Vasco said. "Besides, coming with a large force would guarantee they kill the hostages."

"What about these two?" I asked, pointing to the *nychtera*. "Worth interrogating them?"

"No," Vasco replied, just as quiet. "Couldn't guarantee truth. And if we took the time, others might come. We need to move faster now."

He clapped me on the shoulder. "Up for it, point man?"

"Um, hoo-yah?"

I turned, stretched my awareness ahead of me, and continued

down the tunnel.

Nothing more ahead of us in the way of traps. The tunnel curved a couple of more times. Had a pair of branches, too, but I could feel that those were false leads.

I glanced back at Brikatika though, just to be sure.

Each time Brikatika pointed with one paw down the main tunnel ahead of us.

I nodded. Continued.

The tunnel widened as we went farther. Wide enough we could have walked four abreast comfortably, had we wanted to. And the ceiling was at least sixty feet up now.

The smell of bats got strong enough that my stomach roiled with it.

But we kept going.

Finally, the last length of tunnel before I could feel it open up into a huge, dripping cavern.

I signaled for the others to stick to the tunnel wall as we continued.

Something was wrong, though.

The smell was stronger, yes, but I couldn't really see into the cavern. I couldn't hear any movement or screeing in the cavern ahead either.

Nothing to hear but the sounds of our own movement.

I tried exploring the tunnel entrance with my awareness, and found out why.

Energetic patterns there kept all sounds and sights within. No other traps or tricks to it. Just sensory containment.

That was more than enough, in my opinion. I didn't like it at all.

An effect like that meant there could be hundreds of those great big *nychtera*, all poised and waiting for us to enter. Ready to rip us apart before we even had a chance to offer an objection.

And I had no way of knowing until I crossed that threshold.

I shot Vasco a troubled look. He gave me a grim expression, but nodded for me to continue.

One deep sigh, then I pushed on into the cavern entrance.

29

I STEPPED INSIDE THE CAVERN FROM THE TUNNEL, AND IMMEDIATELY ducked behind a twelve-foot stalagmite to my left.

Nothing pounced.

No great crowd of *nychtera* had been waiting for me to cross the threshold.

I remained un-ripped-apart.

Best news I'd had all day.

Says something about the kind of day I'd been having.

Still. As I got my bearings, I could see that there was more than enough bad news in that cave to go around.

First of all, this place was *huge*.

I'd thought that the prismatic cavern was big. The *nychtera* cavern, deep inside that little tugboat, made the prismatic crystal cavern look like a *snow globe*.

This cavern was easily a mile across, lengthwise, and at least half-that in width.

Heck, the *roof* had to be at least a half-mile up. Far enough away that I would have had to try, if I'd wanted to gauge the exact distance. I couldn't just sense it offhandedly, the way I could sense so many things now.

That roof was far enough away that if those stalactites I could pick out up there fell, they'd reach terminal velocity on the way down. They'd hit this dirty, rocky cavern floor and explode like fragmentation grenades.

And that was only one little worry in that huge cavern.

All over that ceiling were *nychtera*. Couldn't judge how many. Not at this distance. And especially not the way they bundled in and hung there, or crawled across each other.

Hundreds though. Maybe even thousands. And at least half of them filled the air with chirps and screeches and cries.

Their droppings fell indiscriminately. Even if I lived through this, my nice silk shirt was definitely a goner.

That wasn't the worst news though.

Something had heard me come through. Felt, maybe. Couldn't be sure yet. All I knew for certain was that I heard a scuttling somewhere off to my left.

And whatever was doing that scuttling was *big*.

I heard the others come through the cavern entrance behind me. I glanced back to see Vasco, Magellan, even Brikatika slip through and duck behind a different stalagmite. This one on the right-hand side of the entrance.

I hadn't been sure Brikatika should have been allowed to come through. Not until we knew it was safe. But either the big *dorach* wouldn't hear of standing by while his mate and offspring were under threat, or Vasco'd thought we'd need him to find said mate and offspring.

If so, Vasco had a point. Might be able to search for—

"Down!" Vasco yelled.

I dropped to the hard, rocky surface without thinking.

A strand of web the size of my forearm shot past me.

I'd been watching the ground. Should've been watching the walls.

I clambered behind my shielding stalagmite and looked.

Calling it a spider didn't do this thing justice.

This was the King Kong of spiders.

Milky white. Body easily twenty feet from pincers to spinneret.

And its legs looked like cranes, they were so long. Even arched up so its thorax could throw webs our direction...

It was still throwing webs...

"Scatter!" I yelled, but Vasco one-upped me. While I dove away from the spreading filaments, he pulled a Molotov cocktail out of his duffel bag.

He lit the rag with a gesture, and broke the bottle in the center of that web.

Whatever he'd put inside that...

The moment I wondered, the information came flooding to me. A recipe for liquid fire. Not Greek fire, or napalm, or any kind of imitation. Not even plasma or lava.

No.

This was a recipe for fire made liquid. Pure, elemental stuff. Burned a brilliant blue-white, and left even the air in its wake smelling purified and clean.

And that fire spread faster than I could have dreamed. *Whuffed* up all the filaments around me.

That fire spread up the web, racing toward the thorax of the panicking and retreating spider.

The spider scuttled for the ceiling. Desperate to escape. Followed by a dozen much smaller spiders I'd overlooked, I'd been so focused on the giant. These smaller spiders were no larger than, say, motorcycles. But all were just as panicked.

None of them had a chance.

The fire jumped the distance from the end of the web to the Kong spider's thorax.

And just like that, the great white spider vanished in a blazing white puff. Not even ash or smoke left behind.

I didn't know if any of the smaller spiders were caught by the flame. But what survivors I *could* see wanted nothing more to do with us. They were heading for far off corners of the cavern at their top speed.

And those spiders could move.

I let out a breath I hadn't realized I'd been holding. Felt like my heart started beating again. I gave Vasco a twitchy smile.

"I will never, *never* say another bad thing about your duffel bag."

"When did you diss my duffel?" Vasco said, then chuckled. "Sadly, I only have the one of those at the moment. Used the other two yesterday on a..."

Vasco's words trailed off the moment we both realized something.

The *nychtera* had grown silent.

He and I looked up at the same moment.

Hundreds, no *thousands* of brown and yellow eyes looked down at us.

And it might have been nerves, but I thought I saw hatred in every pair of eyes.

"We're doomed," Brikatika said.

"*Where is your mate?*" Vasco snapped at him.

"Far left quadrant of the cavern," Brikatika said without thinking.

The *nychtera* started taking to the air. All of them screeching challenges at us.

"Go!" Vasco barked at me, shoving my shoulder. "Both of you. Stick to the cavern wall."

"What about the—"

"Leave them to us!" Vasco said, followed by a word I couldn't parse. A moment later, I wasn't even sure I'd heard it.

But Magellan heard it. He started growing at speeds that would have made Clifford the Big Red Dog jealous.

I didn't stay to watch though. I started hustling along the side of the cavern, fists up and ready. Couldn't go full speed though. I had to stay slow enough for Brikatika to...

The *dorach* bolted past me.

"*Come on!*" he said in his native tongue.

No time even to frown at that. I just doubled my pace. Still not exactly a sprint, but the two of us were moving along at a pretty good clip.

I couldn't resist glancing back.

Magellan, sixty feet tall, at the least. Swiping paws through the air and knocking whole squadrons of *nychtera* to the ground.

The most impressive thing? Didn't look like he was killing any of them. Knocking them out, sure, but I'd been worried about getting splattered in bat blood and juices.

Not to worry. They thumped here and there, and fell, but made no gruesome snapping sounds. And they didn't bleed at all.

Brikatika and I had to duck around a few fallen *nychtera* as we made our way around the edge of the cavern. Sure looked like they were breathing.

Tough bastards.

Couldn't be sure about the ones Vasco himself was fighting. And anytime a *nychter* was stupid enough to close with him, he pounded the daylights out of it.

"Look out!" Brikatika cried.

Apparently a squadron of *nychtera* had realized that Vasco and Magellan weren't alone.

A dozen of those huge, yellow-and-black bat-things. All winging down at us.

I jumped between Brikatika and the descending *nychtera*, over his protests.

I became a whirlwind of punches and kicks, each strike backed by energies, just like when I'd fought the *gossaks*. Didn't have to think about it. Just trained reflexes.

Moments later, there were twelve unconscious *nychtera* and Brikatika and I were running again. Brikatika was looking at me differently now. Impressed, maybe.

Another squadron came down after us. This batch, alas, was more organized than the last. I took down about eight, but the last four grabbed me and took wing.

Brikatika jumped up. Dug his teeth into the leather of a wing and ripped for all he could. Jaw muscles supplemented by his own weight and his tearing forepaws.

That wing tore right in half. The *nychter* had to let me go as it fell, screaming and bloody, to the rocky surface of the cavern floor.

The other three carrying me made the mistake of looking down.

I caught them between wing-beats. Pulled in with all my muscles and energies, slamming their bodies into one another.

Not enough to knock them out, but enough to knock them out of the air. And we were about fifty feet up at that point.

I surfed one down with my feet, and held the other two in front of me with my hands while the floor got closer...

Closer...

I let go with my hands at the last moment, but it was way too late for them to pull out of the dive, even if they could have.

Three more unconscious *nychtera*, and I was rolling to my feet and running once more, Brikatika beside me.

Magellan barked a challenge that boomed through the cavern. He came trotting over near us to ram any more *nychtera* that were thinking of feasting on *dorach* or Eagleson.

But then came a bat cry louder and sharper than any I'd ever heard before. So loud and sharp that I could feel it in my teeth, in the bones of my skull. All throughout my body.

I'm pretty sure that's when my ears started bleeding.

Looking back, I was lucky that I didn't go deaf right then. My ears were ringing pretty badly though, and kept ringing for quite a while.

I had a fleeting thought of applying Serpent's Kiss inside my ears, then decided no, I could still hear well enough.

Brikatika stumbled, overwhelmed by the sound.

The signal, I should say. Because all the conscious *nychtera*, of which there were still hundreds, all took to the air and retreated to the ceiling.

"Enough!" Chiron's voice,speaking English, but only just loud enough for me to hear over the ringing in my ears.

I could see him now. Standing upright on the rocky floor. Maybe five hundred feet away from me. Two other *nychtera* his size stood with him.

The two beside him held *doracha*. One held a larger *dorach*, the other held two smaller *doracha*.

"Surrender Brikatika," Chiron called out, "or we will kill his mate and offspring."

"*Attention,*" Vasco called out in the screeching language of the *nychtera.* "*We are Locksmiths, and here on official business. Your leader stands in violation of the Va-a-naska Treaty on at least three counts, possibly as many as a dozen.*"

"*Hear him not!*" Chiron ordered his people.

Vasco kept going.

"*As Lockmaster, I am duly informing you that his holding those doracha is itself a violation, as is the threat against their lives that you yourselves heard. Any who stand with him now will be treated as accomplices.*"

Nychtera took wing in droves, over the orders to return shouted by their leader.

True, many *nychtera* remained in support of Chiron, but the greater number left.

"We are still numerous enough to devour you all," Chiron said, English once again.

"Maybe," I said, walking closer. "Maybe not. But it's not going to come to that."

"Release your prisoners," Vasco said. "Turn yourselves in now and it will go easier for you. So far, none of you have died."

"And no one *has* to die here today."

"Keep walking and you'll kill them," Chiron said, but he sounded nervous to me.

Then again, I'd think most sane creatures would feel nervous, when confronted with two Locksmiths and a sixty-foot-tall Beagle.

I smiled. I saw my opening. *Nychtera* might not have been the most honorable creatures around, but their society revolved around pride.

"You are such a coward," I said, shaking my head.

Chiron's brown eyes seemed to light up with inner fire.

"What did you say?"

I chuckled at that. True, I was chuckling at the irony of his asking what I'd said, when I was the one having trouble hearing after that screech he'd let out earlier.

"I called you a *coward*," I said. "Yesterday you tried to straight up murder me, when I had no more defenses to call on than Brikatika's mate and offspring."

I spread my arms out wide. "Now I stand before you. But you must hide behind poor, innocent *doracha*."

"He's right," Vasco said, as though realizing something important. "You *are* a coward."

He laughed a lot louder than my little chuckle.

"To think," he said, still laughing, "the mighty *nychtera* being led by a *coward*."

The two eight-foot-tall *nychtera* on either side of Chiron gave him considering looks. I heard what I thought were jeers coming from the ceiling, but with my ears as they were, I couldn't be sure.

I did notice a few dozen more *nychtera* fly off from the ceiling and leave.

"And what of you?" Chiron said, trying for a mocking tone. "You hide behind a Lockmaster and a giant dog."

"Release those *doracha* and I'll fight you right now."

Sure, I *sounded* confident. Truth was, I didn't know if I could take him. But getting those prisoners released was worth the risk.

"No," called the *nychter* behind Chiron on his right. "Defeat Chiron and we will surrender the *doracha* and submit."

Chiron hissed and screeched in anger at the two behind him. No words I could pick out, until he turned back to me.

"Fine!" Chiron said. "The two of us then!"

And for the second time in two days, the great bat creature leapt into the air, murder in his eyes.

Maybe I should have thought this tactic through...

30

I HAD A FLEETING MOMENT TO WONDER WHAT KATY WOULD THINK, IF she could have seen me right then.

Standing in a huge stone cavern, concealed inside a little tugboat, sailing down the Willamette River south of Oregon City.

Standing ready to fight to my death against an eight-foot-tall, yellow-furred, black-winged bat creature. In defense of a family of oversized talking otters.

The thought pissed me off.

If I was going to die today, I didn't want to do it with Katy in my thoughts. So instead I allowed myself to marvel for a moment at how weird my life had gotten in the last forty-eight hours, and then focused on the fight itself.

Appropriate that I was having the biggest fight of my life in a venue big enough to fit multiple Major League ballparks.

My fight had an audience, too. Crowds of *nychtera* on the cavern ceiling high above. Two more holding hostages — Brikatixa's mate and offspring.

That was Chiron's cheering section, and the moment he took wing, the air filled with screeches and chirps of encouragement.

Well, many of them were also ... letting go from excitement, and the falling guano made the dry air smell worse than any sporting arena I'd ever been to.

My own cheering section — Vasco, Magellan, and Brikatika — tried shouting encouragements too. But honestly, I could only really hear Magellan's.

My ears were still ringing from that painful screech earlier, but the barking of a sixty-foot-tall beagle is hard to miss.

"Assert your dominance, Scott!"

It doesn't sound quite so ... creepy in Doggerel.

All of that, though, I was only aware of in the background. Same way I was aware of my pounding heartbeat, the sweat on my brow, the tension through my muscles, the flood of energies and adrenaline preparing me to fight for my life.

My main focus was on Chiron.

My eyes locked with his hateful brown orbs.

His powerful wings cut through the air the way I cut through water when I had a speed boost.

A hundred feet and closing.

Fifty feet and closing.

Twenty feet and closing. I could smell the blood on his breath now.

He let out another ear-piercing screech.

That one was too much for me. Blew out my eardrums and left me stone deaf.

Ruined the strike I'd been planning. But I did manage to duck under his reaching claws.

Good. Those claws carried some kind of poison. I remembered their fiery, spreading pain all too well from our last encounter.

Chiron flew past. Cut a tight arc straight up into the air and came back at me while I was still rolling to my feet.

So I used the movement to my advantage. Turned the roll into a leaping strike. My body a spear.

I tagged him in the gut. Both fists, backed by energy and momentum. It was like leaping into a furry side of beef fist-first, but I felt him give.

I landed. Whirled. Fists up and ready.

Chiron was still in the air.

Chiron pulled a kind of somersaulting turn in mid-air. Arced high. Mouth moving like he was trying to taunt me.

Joke was on him. I couldn't hear him.

I could feel the breeze his wings kicked up though, as he swooped down away from me, then back up. Building speed in his odd, fluttery flying pattern.

I kept my stance, right where I was. Turned with him. Gauged his speed. Tried to guess his approach.

I'd seen him come at me twice. Both times he arced back up into the air.

False strike this time. He swooped down, but juked right before he came close enough for my leaping kick.

He flipped around in the air. Came back at me twice as fast. No idea how he could do that. Didn't seem possible.

Then he was on me. No time to think. Only react.

But I was a Locksmith for a reason.

Just before his claws could grab me, I spun in place and jumped through a portal, aiming for a spot in the air about thirty feet up and twenty-five feet away.

So many calculations, done so fast in my head. All of them might as well have been done by feel. My ability to sense space turned into an ability to assess speed. To estimate angles.

I leaped through a small, red and green swirling portal...

...and came out in mid-air...

...right above Chiron.

I grabbed his back fur with both hands. Clung to the hot, musky fur.

Chiron barrel-rolled in midair, trying to shake me, but I clung all the tighter.

I tried kicking his wings, but my strike bounced off.

I started laughing. I couldn't hear myself, but I could feel the sound bubbling out of me.

This was wild. A better ride than any roller coaster I'd ever been on, and I'd ridden them all, as often as I could.

I think I whooped. Couldn't be sure though.

I know Chiron was somehow managing to get even angrier at me. I could see it in the way he jerked his head around, trying to figure out if he could bite me.

No good there.

So he switched tactics.

He turned us back down toward the floor. Right now at a height of about a quarter-mile. And he started speeding toward that fatal, rocky surface.

No.

He couldn't be trying to ram.

The guy wasn't immortal. No *nychter* was. He'd never survive that crash either.

He started rolling in the air again. Got me clenching tight. Clinging to his fur.

Then he yanked his wings in and somersaulted.

Once.

Twice.

Three times.

While still barrel-rolling, thanks to his momentum.

I admit it. For all my training, I was good and dizzy now.

Looking back, I like to think the dizziness was a side-effect of the damage to my inner ears.

Either way, I started throwing up all over his fur.

Worse, I was having trouble keeping my grip.

And the ground was coming at us awfully fast.

He spread his wings all at once, but he'd managed to flip over.

I was underneath him now. And he was levelling out his flight.

He was going to scrape me off along the floor.

No choice then. I'd been hoping to somehow use his flight against him. Now trying to do that might prove fatal.

I gritted my teeth. Said a small prayer to any gods that might have watched over Locksmiths.

And I let go with one hand.

Stupid. I know. But I didn't have a whole lot of choice. It was the only way I could make the gesture to open a portal.

"*Alethia.*" No idea if I whispered it or screamed it. Since I couldn't hear myself, all I could do was force my lips and tongue to go through the motions.

And I opened the biggest portal I could. Bright cobalt blue. Smelling of roses. Frizzing with electrical tension.

And I opened it maybe ten feet in front of Chiron. No way he could evade it, not even as agile as he was in the air.

We soared right into that portal—

—and came out in the long hallway under Mount Hood. The strains of Mozart's twenty-fifth symphony filled the air, along with the faint scent of roses.

The two of us came to a gentle halt, right there on the white marble floor. Smack in the middle between the brown stucco walls, with their strips of rose-covered wallpaper, running the length of the walls at waist height.

See, that was why I didn't try using a portal as an attack earlier. Sure, I would have loved to open up a portal in front of the zooming *nychter* and have him pop out right in front of the cavern wall. Knock himself unconscious and win the fight.

Nice and easy, right?

Wrong.

Travel by portal kills momentum.

So when Chiron and I came through into that hallway, we were going no faster than if we'd taken a slow, casual step.

But I expected that. And he didn't.

As we passed through that portal, I let go of the back of his fur with both hands.

The instant we arrived on that red runner carpet, I slammed both fists into the back of his skull, with every erg of power I could put behind the blow.

I staggered him.

I dropped to the carpet and took two steps back, putting my back against that heavy oak door at the near end of the hallway. Started running.

Chiron tried to take wing, but failed. He'd tried to go straight up, as though he were still in the enormous cavern. Too dazed from my blow to realize he could have gone straight forward.

Not enough room, when the ceiling was only ten feet up, and the walls were only seven feet apart.

Cramped as the conditions were here, even if Chiron could take wing, he wouldn't have been able to continue his aerial attacks on me.

Which was the whole point.

Chiron put it all together just a little too slow.

He turned around just in time to intercept my best flying kick. The one that lassoed him with energy, and accelerated me right into his torso at amazing speeds.

That knocked him to the floor.

But the tough bastard wasn't out yet.

I tried for another kick while he was down. He grabbed my foot. Tried to bite me.

Before he could, I kicked him with the other foot.

He let go. Shook his head.

I didn't let him start to rise. I jumped in to start beating on him.

It was a trick.

He tucked in his claws and raked the front half of my body, collar-bone to belly. Tore my good silk shirt to ribbons and opened me like a letter.

No.

He didn't.

Pain all through my body, but I could feel myself laughing. Yes, he'd raked the holy hell out of my front. But my guts stayed right where they were. Sometime during the fight, I'd set up my own ener-getic line of defenses.

Not enough to keep him from hurting me. But definitely enough to keep him from gutting me.

Just another little surprise for old Chiron. One he wasn't ready for.

Now I was inside his defenses. So I turned every bit of that pain into fury, and started pounding away at him while the fiery pain of his poisonous claws spread down my body.

Chiron fell to the marble floor. I hit him a few more times to make sure he was out.

Somewhere in there I felt a portal open, but I didn't have time to worry about that. I kept punching.

Only when I was sure Chiron was out did I allow myself to collapse onto the cool marble floor beside him.

31

THE DISTANT SOUNDS OF A MOZART SYMPHONY TOLD ME I WASN'T dead. Not that I think there's no music in the afterlife. I just think the performances would be better.

This was his fortieth symphony, and I thought the violins were overdoing it a tad, and that the conductor needed to...

Wait. When did I learn so much about...

Oh. Right. Zarindaro. The African man with the ritual scarring on his cheeks, and the complete lack of patience if my attention drifted during his lessons.

Zarindaro had insisted that learning classical music was critical to the development of a Locksmith. Taught us to appreciate the subtleties of the audio side of the energies we worked with.

So I was alive. And awake.

My teeth were gritted against the expectation of pain. Took me a moment to realize that my body wasn't screaming in agony.

I could feel some coolness to the air, along with the faint scent of roses. Enough sensation to tell me I ... was I in a robe? A blanket?

I knew whatever surface I lay on was soft enough. That was something.

Wait.

Sound!

I could hear!

That got me sitting up so fast the robe fell open to the waist. It was white and fluffy and generic in the way that it probably had a hotel logo on it somewhere.

I was sitting on a softly glowing, white crystal couch on the bottom level of Locksmith Central: the big, prismatic crystal cavern.

I just couldn't think of it as huge anymore. Not after that *nychtera...*

"He's awake! He's awake! He's awake! He's awake!"

Magellan's happy barking, from just below the cushions. He was his normal beagle self again, which I found reassuring.

I reached down to pat his head and his tail started going fast enough to power the whole Portland metro area for a month.

He turned, though, and kept up his litany as he ran off.

I smiled at him as my eyes told me the rest of my situation.

Two small *doracha* — by which I mean they were no bigger than normal otters — were galumphing right at me from over near the enormous table, at speed. Brikatika's offspring.

I hadn't gotten a good look at them before, but I could still tell who they were by their coloring, the pattern of subtle reds in the browns that showed a blend of Brikatika's fur patterns with those of Rakata, his mate.

Brikatika and Rakata were just behind their children, though the adults weren't running. Their whiskers twitched pleasure at me though, and their black eyes smiled.

The smaller *doracha* leaped. Knocked my breath right out of me.

I think one of the happiest moments of my life had to be having two happy young *doracha* paw and nuzzle me while I tried to get my breath back.

I was laughing like a fool by the time Janna and Vasco approached, following Magellan.

A *nychter* was with them. One of the eight-foot-tall variety of bat creatures...

K'lakak. I recognized the subtle patterns of his fur. He'd been Chiron's second...

"Good to see you awake," Janna said, smiling as she stared me right in the bare chest, while Brikatika and Rakata retrieved their young and stayed nearby.

I adjusted the robe. Sat with both feet on the softly glowing, white crystal floor.

"What happened?" I asked. "I remember fighting Chiron—"

"You beat him," Vasco said, smiling. "Interesting trick, pulling him through a portal to someplace he'd be off-balance and wouldn't have room to fly."

K'lakak drummed his fingers on his furry yellow belly, in a gesture I thought indicated disapproval.

"Of course, I wasn't sure where you went," Vasco said. "And I had to find out quick. If the end of the fight wasn't witnessed by Chiron's guards—"

"Then they would have been within their rights to kill the *doracha*," K'lakak said. "At least, as I have been given to understand the situation."

"No," I said, and Vasco and Janna said it at the same time.

Janna, as Lady of Portals, finished the thought.

"If Chiron had killed Scott, it would not have, itself, been a treaty violation. That was the only concession given, when Scott issued the challenge. The standoff would have continued."

K'lakak clashed his teeth together a few times, then spoke.

"Chiron was a fool. He should never have tried his wing at smuggling. He should never have involved *doracha*. He should never—"

"And you knew nothing about any of this?" I asked, not trying to hide my disbelief.

"He claims he was kept in the dark," Vasco said, "and we can't prove otherwise."

"*My* innocence, however, does not absolve the *dorach* of his role," K'lakak said. "He did violate the treaty by smuggling."

"He did," Janna said, the steel in her voice belying the youth of her appearance. "And it is *my* place to address that violation, not yours. Now say what you would say, and then leave."

"Very well." K'lakak stepped closer. Snapped his wings out wide, then tucked them back in. "I lead the *nychtera* of this region now. Not Chiron. And I tell you that Chiron struck a blow to the pride of all *nychtera* through his deeds. Pride you have helped restore by defeating him in single combat."

K'lakak cast a baleful eye toward Janna. "Locksmiths are not allowed to accrue debt, but if you, Scott Angus Eagleson, ever find you have need for anything, the *nychtera* will aid you. This is my word."

Before I could so much as acknowledge that, K'lakak leapt into the air and flew off.

He left through a portal in the green section of wall, high up above.

"Think he means all that?" I asked.

"It's a point of pride to him," Vasco said. "So, yes."

"Think he didn't know about the smuggling?"

"Not a chance," Janna said. "It would be a blow to his pride, if their leader could have pulled off such a big undertaking without his knowing. Problem is, it'd be an even bigger blow to get caught for involvement."

Brikatika stepped up to me then.

"We can never thank you enough for all you have done for us. I owe you for saving my life before you became a Locksmith, but beyond any debts, I would be proud if you counted me a friend."

So much sincerity in those little black eyes that I couldn't speak. I tried to tell him that without words.

He clasped my right hand in both of his, then gave me his awkward attempt at a handshake.

As soon as he finished, Rakata did the same. Then both of their children.

"We are ready," Brikatika said to Janna. "And thank you for allowing us that moment of thanks."

Janna turned and opened a deep blue portal that smelled of melted cheese and sounded like a soprano holding a high C.

One more happy twitch of their whiskers toward me, and the four *doracha* departed.

For a moment, the only sound was the symphony, quiet. Almost respectful.

"Where did you send them?" I asked.

"Venice," Janna said, giving me a big smile.

Magellan barked happily, not saying anything more than expressing happiness.

I laughed as it all came together in my head, and Vasco and Janna smiled as I spoke my thoughts.

"They had to be banished, for Brikatika's role in the smuggling, but he was terrified that if they went away from earth, they'd be found and killed."

"Exactly," Janna said. "The treaty specifies that smugglers are banished. And the general assumption — and precedent — is for banishment to be from this world. But Brikatika helped crack the smuggling ring and take down all of the containment rocks, as well as several dozen *gossaks*."

"When did—"

"The rest of us have been busy while you were recovering," Vasco said.

"How long was I out?"

"Only about three hours," Janna said. "Cleanup was top priority. I put everyone on it."

"So you banished Brikatika from Portland, but not from earth. Clever."

"Thank you," Janna said, fluffing her hair with one hand.

"But what about Chiron?"

"Banished, of course, along with a host of others. And I didn't send them anywhere as nice as Venice."

"Were there any casualties? During the big fight?"

"Wounded, yes," Vasco said. "But none killed."

"How?"

"I'm the best dog in the world!" Magellan barked. "Soft mouth! Soft paws! Me! Me! Me!"

Vasco chuckled and threw the eager beagle a treat as he explained.

"Magellan may not open portals, but he's been through his share of training. Knows how much force to use with a wide variety of races."

"Seven hundred sixty-eight!" Magellan added. "Want me to name them?"

"Not now," Vasco said, but patted Magellan's head as turned back to me. "Plenty of those *nychtera* needed medical treatment, don't get me wrong. But no fatalities."

That gave me a sigh of relief. I still felt bad about the *riskatan*. But a question that had been bugging me bubbled to the surface.

"What were they smuggling, anyway?"

"Emeralds," Vasco said. "Big ones, but not so big they'd draw special attention. Didn't need to move many at a time to make their money—"

"And money wasn't the point anyway," Janna said. "Chiron was building contacts. A network of humans here in the Pacific Northwest, built around a handful he could actually interact with."

"We put a stop to it just in time," Vasco added. "We'll clear that part up too."

"You won't banish the humans," I said, frowning.

"Of course not," Janna said. "They're not signatories of the treaty, and they're not Locksmiths. I'll just ... close their minds to certain details of what they've done and been through."

"Will they be going to jail?"

"For what?" Vasco asked with a shrug. "Emeralds weren't stolen. At least, not on earth. Probably not where they came from either. No crimes against human law have been committed."

"Can't have it though," Janna said. "That kind of smuggling. Play havoc with the jewelry market, and eventually people would start asking the wrong questions, in ways and numbers that would be harder to deal with."

"What about Quelan?" I asked.

"What about Quelan?" Janna repeated, looking at Vasco and making the question sound far more important than I had.

But Vasco only gave me a blank look.

"She made all those hiding places in the rocks," I said. "She made the whole operation possible. So what happens to her?"

"Nothing," Janna said with a grimace. "Not against any treaty to construct space inside an object. Heck, if it were, we wouldn't be allowed to stretch space the way we do in things like Vasco's duffel bag. It's a related effect, and innocent in and of itself."

"The car's manufacturer isn't responsible if the car is used to help rob a bank," I said.

"Exactly," Janna said. "She'll cross us again, I'm sure. But she didn't do it this time."

"I think that brings us to the big question," Vasco said.

"Yes!" Magellan barked, bouncing up and down. "Yes! The big question!"

"Big question?" I asked.

"Well," Janna said, looking away for a moment.

Then she inhaled deeply through her nose, adjusted her thick glasses and looked back at me.

"Technically," she said, "your punishment for accidentally killing the *riskatan* is finished. You make a fine Locksmith, but you were recruited under pressure. So, the big question is, do you want to continue being a Locksmith?"

"What exactly does it involve?" I asked.

"A lot of your time's your own," Vasco said. "So long as you keep an eye on things. Help who needs helping, that kind of thing. Hang with me for a couple of days and I'll show you what I mean, now that we're not under pressure."

"And when a need arises," Janna started, but Vasco interrupted her.

"Which it will. Not infrequently."

"Then I call you in and give you a formal task." Janna smiled then.

"Being a Locksmith carries a stipend, of course. Pretty generous, because money isn't exactly a problem for us."

"And there's camaraderie," Vasco added. "We Locksmiths are a pretty friendly bunch."

"Yeah we are!" Magellan said, still bouncing.

"What happens if I say no?"

"If you say no," Janna said through a sigh, "then I close your mind to the … esoteric details of the last couple of days. You'll think you caught a nasty cold in the river, and stayed in bed fighting a fever. You'll still be able to notice things the way you could before, but—"

I raised one palm and shook it until she stopped talking.

"Doesn't matter," I said, shaking my head. "Don't know why I bothered asking. I'm in. All the way."

"Yes!" Magellan barked.

Vasco clapped me on the shoulder, while Janna shook my hand. Vasco handed me back my clothes. All of them neatly cleaned, pressed and perfect.

Even my good blue silk shirt. Which had been torn to shreds...

"Oh," I said quickly. "One question."

I waited until I had the attention of all three of them.

"I don't suppose there's a less painful way to heal injuries in the field?"

"In the field?" Janna said. "No."

"Well," Vasco said. "Give yourself a paper cut and you'll recall the kind of energetic healing we can do."

"Problem is," Janna said, "anything *beyond* a paper cut requires the kind of focus you won't have, if you're the one wounded."

"And you can't afford, if you aren't," Vasco finished. "Energetic healing in the field leaves you vulnerable to attack."

"Then we'd have *two* wounded Locksmiths." Janna shook her head. "It's no good. Best to stick with Bruisebane and Serpent's Kiss, and watch each other's backs."

Well that sucked.

Still, it was a small price to pay for the whole world of wonders that had opened up to me. Because now I knew the difference between weird and wyrd. Between eccentric behavior, and true magic.

Portland — Portal-Land — had both. So whether it was spelled with an "ei" or a "y," I knew just exactly what kind of weird Portland was.

My kind of weird.

SIGN UP FOR STEFON'S NEWSLETTER

Stefon loves to keep in touch with his readers, and loves to keep you reading. The best way for him to do both is for you to sign up for his newsletter.

Sign up at http://www.stefonmears.com/join

If you sign up for Stefon's newsletter, you get...

- Monthly updates about his publishing and travel schedules
- His latest news, in brief, and answers to reader questions
- A free short story for signing up
- List-only offers and occasional specials
- Plus a free short story every month!

ABOUT THE AUTHOR

Stefon Mears has been known to talk to "otters." Stefon has more than twenty books to his credit, and he never stops writing. He earned his M.F.A. in Creative Writing from N.I.L.A., and his B.A. in Religious Studies (double emphasis in Ritual and Mythology) from U.C. Berkeley. He's a lifelong gamer and fantasy fan. Stefon lives in Portland, Oregon, with his wife and three cats.

Look for Stefon online:
www.stefonmears.com
himself@stefonmears.com